Closer Than Ever

Dedication

For all who read this series

May you know your God
and His incredible love for you.

This I declare of the LORD;
"He alone is my refuge, my place of safety;
He is my God, and I am trusting Him!"

Psalm 91:2

Chapter One

"Sarah Anderson, you can't move!" Brianne whined, falling into her best friend's arms and letting out a fake cry.

"I'm sorry," Sarah said, wrapping her arms around her. "But it's not up to me. My dad got transferred."

"So? Stay here and live with me. It's just your family. You won't miss them."

"Somehow I don't think they'll let me do that," Sarah laughed, stepping back and shaking her head. Her dark brown ponytail swished from side to side. "I'd love to, you know that, but this is going to happen whether or not you or me want it to."

Brianne Carmichael had known about her best friend moving for a month now, but with Sarah leaving in another two days, the reality of it was hitting her harder than ever. Sarah had been the best friend she'd ever had.

Brianne had been born in Salem, the state capital of Oregon, twelve and a half years ago. Her dad, Jacob Carmichael, or Pastor Jake to most, had been the assistant pastor at a large Christian church there at the time. When she was four, her parents, along with herself and her younger brother J.T., had moved to

Sweet Home, a small rural town in the middle of the state. Her dad had been the pastor at a church there for six years before they moved here to Clatskanie in the northwest corner of Oregon, where her dad was the pastor of Rivergate Community Church on the outskirts of the small town.

On her first Sunday there, in November of her fifth grade year, she had met Sarah in the combined Sunday school class of fifth and sixth grade girls and learned Sarah lived on her street. Sarah had been friendly and nice, and they'd hit it off great.

"Okay, enough of this pouting," Sarah said, linking arms with her and heading for the water. "We have today, Bree. Let's have fun, okay?"

"Okay," Brianne said. The moving van wouldn't be pulling away from Sarah's house until Monday morning, and for today they were here at the park with their youth group. Pastor Doug had organized this late summer day for them to swim, hang out, and have a barbecue dinner as a welcome for the new seventh graders joining the group, and she was one of them.

She had been looking forward to joining the youth group along with her friends Sarah, Emily, and Ashlee, who had all been a part of her Sunday school class ever since she had moved here. There were also some boys her age in a separate class, but now they would all be in the youth group together: Tim and Jason, and also Pastor Doug's son Austin. She considered all of the kids her age from church to be her friends, but she was the closest to Sarah. They did everything together.

Brianne and Sarah ran into the cold water in their matching purple bathing suits they had bought together earlier this summer and immediately began a huge water fight with Emily, Austin, and a few others who were standing nearby. Austin retaliated, but he went after Sarah more than her. Brianne knew Austin had a huge crush on Sarah, something Sarah also knew, but thus far she hadn't allowed Austin to be anything besides a good friend.

Sarah wasn't interested in having a relationship beyond friendship with boys yet. Many of them had tried to get her to go to a school dance with them or to the movies, but she didn't even allow them to call her on the phone anymore, ever since one boy from school had mistook a forty-five minute phone conversation as a sign that she liked him.

By the next day at school everyone thought they were together. Sarah had never told him she had any interest in him in that way whatsoever. She had been friendly and sweet, like she was with everyone, but guys seemed to mistake her sweetness for, 'I really like you and want to be your girlfriend.' She was getting pretty tired of it and wasn't looking forward to going to a new school where she would have to spend the first days of her seventh grade year dealing with any of that on top of the usual difficulties of moving.

Brianne sort of envied her though. At least boys were noticing her. She supposed she didn't want a bunch of boys trying to call her and hanging around all the time. She had seen Sarah having a hard time with it, but she thought maybe one would be nice. But right now she had much bigger concerns than what boy, if any, liked her. She needed to find a new best friend she could enjoy being with and talk to as easily as Sarah, but she didn't know how. With Sarah she hadn't done anything to gain her friendship, it had just happened.

Once the water-fight ceased, she and Sarah swam around in the water and then got out to sun themselves on the shore while they waited for dinner to be served. Pastor Doug had the barbecue going, and Brianne could smell the hamburgers and hot dogs cooking. Remembering her mother's words before she left the house today, she told Sarah they should go see if they could help in some way, and they put their shorts and t-shirts on over their mostly dry suits and walked to the picnic area.

"Can we help with something?" Brianne asked Pastor Doug, seeing sacks of buns and other things sitting on the table beside the grill. She had taken her blondish-brown hair out of its ponytail to let her hair dry naturally in the warm sun, but she secured the long strands away from her face once again with a pink band.

"Sure," he said, appearing appreciative of their willingness to help. "You can put all that stuff out. These should be ready soon."

They went to work, and Austin joined them a few minutes later. He was wearing his red swim trunks and had put on a t-shirt. His dark blonde hair was wet, and he hadn't bothered to comb it into place.

Brianne didn't know if his dad had already asked him to help, or if Austin had come over because Sarah was here, but either way she welcomed his arrival. Austin was a lot of fun. He wasn't obnoxious like a lot of the boys her age. He wasn't overly serious either, just fun and nice. He came over to her house a lot along with his younger brother, Calvin, to play video games with her younger brothers, usually on Sunday afternoons and more often during the summer. Other than Sarah, Brianne supposed he was the person she had gotten to know the best during the last two years.

She thought he was cute. His hair color was similar to hers, and he kept it short most of the time. Whenever it began to grow over his ears, as it was currently, it had this little curl to it both she and Sarah thought was adorable but he hated.

"There are more drinks in the truck, Austin," his dad said. "Can you go get them and restock the cooler?"

"Sure," he said somewhat reluctantly, but he went.

Brianne had often felt a special connection with Austin because he was a pastor's kid too. That had grown two weeks ago when they went to summer camp for a week along with their other friends from church. She had been going to the camp since she was little because it was close to where she used to live in Sweet Home. When she moved here, she discovered kids from the church often went there too, and she had continued going with her new friends the past two summers.

Going to junior high camp this year had been different than her previous years because they did crazier games, had more free time, and were spoken to more seriously about their lives and relationship with God. They had a time one morning Brianne had really enjoyed where they were supposed to spend a full hour alone with God. Brianne had gone to sit by the lake to read her Bible, pray, and think about where she wanted to see her life go in the coming year as she entered seventh grade and had her best friend moving away.

Near the end of the hour, just when she was beginning to feel restless and ready to get back to her friends, Austin had come to sit by her. He said he wanted to ask her something, and she told him to go ahead. She thought it was going to be about Sarah, but it wasn't.

"Do you ever wish you were a regular kid?"

"What do you mean?" she laughed. "What do you think I am?"

"I mean that you weren't a pastor's kid?"

"Oh," she said, taking a moment to think about that. She hadn't thought of herself as being different because her dad was a pastor, but she supposed it did set her apart in the minds of others. "Yeah, I guess so. Not that I hate it or anything, but sometimes going to church every week gets a little old, and sometimes I feel like everyone is watching me and expecting me to be perfect."

Austin hadn't replied, and she asked him the same question.

"Why? Do you?"

"I used to," he said. "A lot, actually. But I spent the past hour deciding I'm okay with it. I know there are worse things than having a dad who's a pastor."

"Everyone loves your dad, Austin. He's a great youth pastor."

"Yeah, I know."

"What's so bad about it?"

"Nothing, I guess."

"Do others bug you about it sometimes?"

"Yes."

"Kids at school, or from church?"

"From church mostly."

Brianne hadn't experienced that since she had been here, but her best friend was more into God and reading her Bible and everything than she was. Sarah had never once made fun of her about her dad being a pastor or anything else.

Sarah interrupted Brianne's thoughts. "I'll be right back," she whispered in her ear, heading in the same direction as Austin had gone to get more drinks out of the truck. Brianne wondered what that was about and glanced at Pastor Doug.

He watched Sarah disappear out of sight and then leaned over and said, "Is there something going on there I should know about?"

She laughed. "I have no idea."

Chapter Two

By the time Sarah and Austin returned, most of the group had gathered at the picnic area, and Brianne didn't get a chance to talk to Sarah about her unexplained exit ten minutes ago. Brianne had finished setting out the plates, napkins, cups, and various food items. A couple of the high school girls had come to help also. Brianne didn't mind helping. With four younger siblings, she was constantly helping her mom with dinner and chores around the house. She usually welcomed the break from doing homework and the constant interruptions and questions coming from her little sister. Beth was five, and Brianne loved her, but she never stopped talking sometimes.

Her family laughed about it but never tried to get her to be quiet unless she was using her voice to be bossy. When her parents had adopted Beth out of foster care at age two, she didn't even speak, and she didn't talk much until she was about three and a half. She had been abused as a baby and taken away from her parents. She came to live with them at the age of two as a very broken and fragile little girl. But once she had learned to accept their love and lose the fear of being abused, she had come out of her shell, and now they couldn't get her to stop talking.

Brianne had another younger sibling who was also adopted. Steven was eight and had also been in foster care until he was three when her family had brought him into their home. He hadn't been abused, just abandoned. He had mild autism, and his reclusive and strange behaviors as a toddler had been too much for his young mother to deal with. She had taken him to day care one day and never came back.

When her parents adopted Steven, Brianne had only been seven, but she had loved Steven from the first time she had seen him. Her natural younger brothers, J.T. who was five at the time, and Jeffrey who was three, she thought were pesky. But Steven was so quiet, and his big brown eyes, warm brown skin, and curly black hair had made her want to hold him all the time. He was more like a normal eight-year-old now, and she did sometimes see him as being as obnoxious as Jeffrey and J.T., but he also had a very sweet side to him. He often came to sit beside her on the couch when she was watching television or reading, snuggling up next to her and sitting there quietly.

Brianne waited to get in the food line until Sarah did. Austin was right there too, so she couldn't ask Sarah why she had gone to talk to him. The three of them, along with Emily, Ashlee, Tim, and Jason all sat together once they had their food.

"What are we going to do in youth group this year, Austin?" Ashlee asked.

"How should I know?"

"Your dad is in charge?"

"Yeah, my dad, Ashlee. Not me. If you want to know, ask him."

"Sorry. You don't have to be so rude. I was just asking."

"He's going to talk about it later," Austin replied in a more neutral tone.

Thinking once again of her quest for a new best friend, Brianne wondered if Emily or Ashlee could possibly take Sarah's place. She couldn't really see it with Emily because Emily was homeschooled and really busy with all of her dance, theater, and music. It would be difficult to get together with her during the week. She and Sarah had become close friends because they saw each other every day, not just on Sundays.

She went to school with Ashlee, but Ashlee wasn't an easy person for her to talk to. She was very judgmental and wasn't afraid to let her opinions be known. She was always giving her advice, and most of it was ridiculous. Brianne had overheard Ashlee saying something to Austin earlier about asking his "daddy" if it was okay to go to another area of the park where he could use his skateboard along with Tim and Jason, and Brianne realized Ashlee was one of those who bugged Austin about his dad being a pastor. She had never thought about it before because Ashlee and Austin didn't get along most of the time, but Brianne knew her words probably bothered Austin more than he let on.

Brianne thought of another girl at school who might be a better candidate for a new best friend. Brianne got along well with Marissa, one of her and Sarah's friends. They had similar interests like scrapbooking, swimming, and playing flute in the band at school. But Marissa's family didn't attend the church, and Marissa had a lot of other friends, so Brianne couldn't imagine Marissa needing her friendship or them hanging out together all the time.

After everyone had finished eating their food, Pastor Doug, who was actually only paid as their part-time youth pastor, talked to the group about the upcoming months and things he had planned. They were going on a retreat at the end of September, and they would be having some kind of activity every other Saturday, either in the afternoon or evening. He encouraged the incoming seventh graders to not be afraid to join in, and for the older high school students to not get so busy with work and school activities they stopped coming.

Brianne knew Pastor Doug had been having a difficult time with that the past couple of years because she had heard her mom and dad talking about it. After many years of running a successful, well-attended youth program at the church before her family had moved here, Pastor Doug had convinced the former pastor, the church board members, and the people of the church to build a youth building adjacent to the main church, and they had been raising funds to do it. Construction had begun this spring, and they expected it to be finished by sometime next year, but for some unexplained reason, the youth attendance had taken a nose-dive in the last year or so, and now her dad and Pastor Doug had a lot of people in the church wondering if they really needed the new building.

Brianne hadn't thought much about it, but she realized this was her group now and their building. She said a silent prayer while Pastor Doug was talking that once the building was finished, they would have enough students to fill it up and make good use of it.

The excitement she felt about what would lie ahead for her in the coming months made her momentarily forget about Sarah moving on Monday and what Sarah had wanted to talk to Austin about earlier. It wasn't until they arrived back at the church she remembered. While they waited for her mom to come pick them up, Brianne asked her about it. Austin was helping his dad take things from the truck inside the church.

"I just wanted to tell him I will miss him, and that of all the guys who let me know they wanted me to be their girlfriend or whatever, I had the hardest time saying no to him."

"Really?" she said. "You didn't tell me that."

"I know. I guess I thought maybe in a couple of years I would consider it if he was still interested, but now I'm not going to have that chance. I just wanted him to know I do think he's different than other guys and to tell him not to change—he's great the way he is, and someday he'll make a great boyfriend for the right girl."

Brianne hadn't thought much about boys and dating yet, and she knew that was a few years away for her, but Sarah was right. Austin was special, and she felt another spontaneous prayer form in her heart that he would find the right girl at the right time. Someone sweet like Sarah. Someone absolutely perfect for him.

***

"Which color do you want?" Sarah asked, holding up three bottles of nail polish. "Icy pink, dark pink, or aquamarine?"

"The light pink," she said. "I'm going to wear my pink skirt to church tomorrow."

"Which one?" Sarah asked with a laugh. "You have about five!"

"Nuh-uh," she defended herself. "I only have three, and that one I got for my birthday barely fits me anymore. I'm getting too tall."

Brianne loved pink, and purple was a close second. Her room, where they were currently giving each other manicures before Sarah had to go home tonight, was mostly pink and lavender. Her curtains, walls, and bedding were the light shade of purple, and her comforter was both pink and lavender in a swirly tie-dye pattern. She had received it for her twelfth birthday last February, and she loved it.

They sat on the floor and painted one another's nails. Hers pink, Sarah's aquamarine. For as much as she loved pink, Sarah was equally partial to just about any shade of blue imaginable.

"What's your room at your new house like?" she asked, setting the bottles of polish back on her dresser while they waited for their nails to dry.

"It's big," Sarah said, moving from the floor to sit on the bed. "Way bigger than the one I have now. When we went to look at the house, the girl who lived there had a full-sized bed, two dressers, and a desk, and there was still plenty of floor space; and the closet is huge with those white organizers in them, you know like Ashlee has in her room?"

"So, if I wanted to come visit you sometime, there would be plenty of space for me?"

"Definitely," she laughed. "Are you going to come sometime?"

"If you want me to. My mom said it was okay."

"Of course I want you to," she said. "I'm really going to miss you, Bree. You're the best friend I've ever had."

"I am?" she asked, not knowing why that surprised her, but it did.

"Yes!" Sarah blasted. "Before you moved here, I had nobody I could talk to and have fun with like I do with you."

"What about Ashlee and Emily?"

"We were friends, but not like this. Ashlee drives me crazy most of the time, and Emily is so busy. I mostly only saw her on Sundays, not every day of the week like you."

For the past three weeks, Brianne had been thinking about losing her best friend and letting her disappointment be known loud and clear. Sarah had been more calm about it, and Brianne had assumed moving away wasn't as big of a deal to her, but the look on Sarah's face told her she was wrong.

"Are you scared?" she asked.

"Terrified," Sarah said.

Brianne sat beside her on the edge of the bed and gave her a hug. They held each other for a long time, and Brianne was surprised when Sarah began to cry. Sarah rarely cried.

"It'll be okay," she said. "You're a great person, Sarah. Everyone instantly likes you. Just be yourself."

Sarah didn't respond until she released her and grabbed a tissue. Sarah thanked her and let out a huge sigh. "A year ago I wouldn't have been so scared, but now with all this boy-stuff going on, I feel like I can't be myself. Guys take it the wrong way. What am I supposed to do?"

"Keep saying no like you've been doing here."

"Yeah, I guess. If I knew it was going to be like this, I would have preferred to stay ten forever."

"But when we were ten, we were wishing we were twelve," she laughed.

Sarah laughed too and gave her another hug. "I will miss you, Brianne. Write me, okay?"

"I will, and you write me back and tell me everything." Brianne reached for some lollipops she had on her desk and let Sarah pick one.

Sarah smiled. "Will you pray for me?"

Brianne realized she had never prayed for Sarah before. She seemed like the kind of person who didn't need prayer. She was strong in her faith and seemed to have it all together. Her parents were happy, and other than the last few months with boys being eager to spend time with her, she hadn't had any major problems in her life. But Brianne knew Sarah needed her love and support, and she was happy to give it.

"Yes, I'll pray for you," she said, selecting a pink lollipop for herself and removing the wrapper. "And pray for me too, okay? You're the best friend I've ever had, and it's going to be really, really hard without you here."

Chapter Three

Brianne spent most of Sunday with Sarah, first at church in the morning, and then at Sarah's house that afternoon. She helped her with last-minute packing and had dinner with her family. Sarah's family had always welcomed her into their home, and she wondered what family would be living here in their place.

After dinner, Sarah's older brother, Scott, who was sixteen and had his driver's license, drove them into Longview to see a movie—one they had wanted to see ever since it came out last week, but they had waited until tonight. They shared a tub of buttery popcorn, and the movie was funny with a good message about friendship, and it helped Brianne to enjoy her last night with Sarah instead of sulking about her moving tomorrow.

After the movie, while they waited for her mom to come pick them up in front of the theater, a couple of guys from school came outside and were about to walk past them when one of them spotted Sarah and turned to say hello.

"Hey, Sarah," Brady said as if she would be thrilled to see him. "What movie did you see?"

Sarah told him. Brianne could tell she was trying to act casual and as disinterested in seeing him as possible without being completely rude. Sarah didn't have it within herself to go that far. Brianne had never seen her be anything but nice to anyone.

"Did you like it?" Brady asked, laughing a bit at their choice.

"Yes," she said. "It was funny."

Brady was the guy from school who had pursued Sarah during the last few weeks of their sixth-grade year and she had the forty-five minute phone conversation with. After that he had called her every night for a week until she asked him not to, but it hadn't stopped him from talking to her at school and asking her out all the time. She told him repeatedly she wasn't allowed to date yet, but when he suggested she meet him somewhere without her parents knowing about it, she had been more honest and told him she wasn't interested. Brady was very good looking, and most girls would die to be asked out by him, but Sarah thought he was arrogant, rude, and selfish. Brianne agreed, but he was rather cute, she thought.

Brady pointed to a movie-poster on the side of the theater advertising a movie currently showing. "Have you seen that? It's really good."

"My parents won't let me," Sarah replied.

"So? Do you want to meet me here sometime?"

"Sorry, I can't," Sarah said. Brianne wondered why she didn't tell Brady she was moving, but she didn't interrupt, letting Sarah handle this on her own. Brianne had no idea what to say anyway.

"Come on," he pressed, putting his arm around her shoulders. "I'll let you bring your friend along."

"Her name is Brianne," she said.

"She's cute too," he said as if he'd never met her before. She had been in the same grade with him for the past two years. "Danny will come too, and we can make it a double date."

Brady's friend Danny glanced at her and winked. Brianne had never been so glad to see her mom drive up. Sarah saw the van too, and they both stepped away. Sarah didn't say anything else to Brady, and they got into the side door without looking back.

"Everything all right back there?" her mom asked.

"Yeah," Sarah answered. "Just Brady and Danny who think they are sooo cool."

"Why didn't you tell him you're moving?" Brianne asked her.

"And have him ask for my new phone number? No thanks."

Brianne laughed. "You're so smart. I never would have thought of that until it was too late."

Sarah leaned over and whispered something in her ear. "Promise me something?"

"What?"

"Promise me you won't go out with guys like Brady and Danny once they start asking you?"

She laughed. "I don't think that day will ever come."

"It will, Bree. Promise me?"

She laughed again. "Not gonna happen, but I promise."

"I'm serious."

"I know. I said I promise."

Sarah sat back and said nothing more on the subject. When they got to Sarah's house, her mom pulled into the driveway, and Brianne got out of the van to give Sarah a hug. Neither of them said anything for a minute. It had all already been said.

"I had fun tonight," Brianne said. "Talk to your parents about coming on the retreat next month, okay?"

"I will," she said. "And you write."

"I will."

"I love you, Bree. I'll miss you so much."

"I love you too."

Sarah stepped back and waved as she walked up the path and opened the door. Once she had disappeared inside, Brianne turned away and went back to the van, getting into the front seat beside her mom.

It only took one sympathetic look from her to make Brianne burst into tears. "Why do they have to move, Mama? It's not fair!"

"I know, honey," she said, stroking her hair and letting her cry. "I'm sure God has His reasons, but I know it's hard."

Her mom backed out of the driveway onto the country road and headed for their house. By the time she had driven up the long driveway and turned off the van, Brianne's tears had subsided, but she felt very sad. And she was mad at God.

She had felt this way two years ago when her parents had decided to move here. She'd had several good friends in Sweet Home, and moving to a new church and school had been a scary experience for her. She knew God had turned her fear into joy last time when she met Sarah, but she had a difficult time imagining any friend could replace her. Why did things have to change? Why did God give her such a good friend if He was going to take her away?

Brianne went to her room once they were inside, and she wrote a letter to Sarah right then, sharing all of her current thoughts. Beth was sleeping in the bed across the room. Brianne had been sharing a room with her little sister for about a year now. When Beth had first come to live with them, she couldn't sleep alone and had slept with her mom and dad until they could get her to sleep in a crib in their room. She hadn't outgrown it until last summer. Sometimes Beth crawled in bed with her in the middle of the night now, but not always.

In the morning Brianne slept in, got up to take a shower, had some cold cereal, and then moped around the house. School didn't start until next week, and she had no idea what she was going to do with the last week of her summer. Going outside before lunchtime, she called her cats and waited for them to come from wherever they were napping. Underneath the front porch was their favorite place in the summertime, and they both came sauntering out after a few moments.

Molly first, her two year old orange tabby, and then Whiskers whom she'd had since she was eight.

Molly preferred to lie on her side in the warm sun and have her fluffy orange and white fur stroked. Whiskers came to rub his black and gray striped fur against her leg and then eventually crawled into her lap and let her scratch the top of his head between his large ears. Whiskers had been the first pet she'd ever had, and she loved both of her cats very much. They had a way of comforting and calming her whenever she felt overwhelmed or sad, and today she felt both. She hadn't told anyone so, but she was nervous about going into seventh grade, and now it was only a week away.

That afternoon Austin came over to play video games with her brother. J.T. was ten and would be entering fifth grade this year. Jeffrey and Steven had gone on a camping trip with the third and fourth grade boys from church, and Austin's brother, Calvin, who was eleven, had gone fishing with his dad today, or they would have been here playing too.

When J.T. had to go help Mom with something, Austin invited her to play because it was better as a two-person game. Brianne had played video games some in the past, but not much recently. Normally she would have declined the offer, but she was bored and didn't have anything better to do.

Austin taught her how to play the game, and she picked it up quick. He was much better at it than she was, but she did all right.

"Not bad for a girl," Austin said after he beat her.

"Thanks," she said, taking it as a compliment.

"Missing Sarah pretty bad, huh?"

"What makes you say that?"

"You're playing video games with me."

She laughed. "Would you like me to paint your nails now?"

"No, thanks," he said. "Let's go another round."

J.T. returned and wanted his controller back, but Austin told him to let her have another turn. "I can beat her," he joked.

Brianne played one more time and then handed it back to J.T., but she remained in the room and watched them. Remembering what Sarah had said about Austin on Saturday, Brianne knew she was right. Austin was nothing like Brady and Danny. He was attracted to Sarah just as much as the next guy, but he had approached her in a respectful way, not suggesting they meet somewhere secretly or even asking her out, but just letting her know he would like to hang out with her sometimes away from school and church—like playing video games at his house or asking her to come watch him at the skate park.

Sarah had told him she only wanted to be friends and see each other in ways they normally would, and Austin had respected her decision, hanging around her a little more at school and at church, but not to the point where he was being obnoxious about it.

Not that she expected him to, but Brianne wondered what she would do if Austin ever asked her the same thing. Would she want to spend time with him in ways outside of their normal friendship like they did now? She never minded him coming over to play video games with her brothers, and she enjoyed going to school and church with him. Would he ever look at her the way he looked at Sarah? And would she want him to?

For now, she thought it would be weird. Austin was just Austin. A good friend. Someone she could be herself with. She didn't want that to change any more than she wanted Sarah to move away. She wasn't ready to be with boys like that. She thought it would be nice for a boy to notice her for once, but deep down she didn't feel ready for it.

Chapter Four

Brianne received three letters from Sarah that week. The first two were mostly informative: 'We made it. We're getting moved in. My room is huge!' But the third one that came on Saturday was more heart-to-heart.

Dear Brianne,

It's Thursday night, and it's starting to feel like home here, I guess. We met our neighbors who live across the street today, and they seem nice. They remind me of your family, but they don't have any kids my age. There's a girl who's fifteen and a boy that's seventeen and a younger boy who is ten. They go to church and invited us to come to theirs this Sunday, so we'll probably go there and check it out.

I also went to register for school today, signed up for my classes, got assigned to a locker, and took a tour of the school. It's nice. It was built a couple of years ago, so everything is new. They have a huge library with really nice computers, and a three-court gym. I miss you terribly. I sure hope God knows what He's doing too, and I'm sure He does, but it's kind of hard to see that right now. I know what you're saying about wondering why things can't stay the same, but I guess they can't for reasons we don't know yet.

One thing I was thinking is even though I know there will be guys like Brady here, I think I'll be more prepared to handle them right. I gave Brady too much in the beginning—letting him call me and talking to him when I should have shut it down in the first place. He surprised me, and I guess I sort of enjoyed the attention at first, but now I know better. I know I need to wait for guys like Austin and let them know I just want to be friends for now.

The more I think about it, the more I know I'm not ready for any of that. My parents told me they don't think it's a good idea for me to date until I'm at least sixteen, but they aren't going to forbid me to. They want me to make my own decision about it once I'm in high school, but I think that's what I'm going to decide for myself. What's the point of dating some guy when I'm fourteen? What am I going to do, date him for eight years until I marry him? It seems dumb to me. I think we should both decide to wait until we're sixteen. What do you think?

Well, enough about boys! I don't want to talk about it anymore. You're praying for me, right? School starts on Tuesday. I signed up for choir, and I think I'm going to try out for volleyball. Those will both be good ways to meet people, and you can bet I'm going to be on the lookout for someone like you. I need a friend like you, Bree. Someone who won't try to push me into doing things I don't want to do, or who blabs my secrets to everyone, or gives me terrible advice like you-know-who. Pray for that for me, and I'll be praying the same for you.

Friends Forever,
Sarah

"This I declare of the LORD; 'He alone is my refuge, my place of safety; He is my God, and I am trusting Him!" Psalm 91:2

Brianne wanted to write Sarah back right away, but Beth had been begging her to read a book to her ever since she had returned from the mailbox, so she set Sarah's letter aside, took the book from Beth, and read the story to her twice. When she finished, Beth hugged her tightly around the middle and said, "I love you, Bree."

"I love you too, sweetie."

"Did you read your letter?"

"Yes, I did."

"Who was it from?"

"Sarah."

"I miss Sarah," she said.

"Me too."

"Is she going to come back?"

"No. Maybe to visit, but not to stay."

Sarah hadn't mentioned anything in her letters about going on the retreat next month, and Brianne hoped she could go, but she decided she wasn't going to ask her about it again. If Sarah wanted to go, she would.

She wrote Sarah back that night before she went to bed. The first part of her letter was more generic about what she had done this week—new clothes she had gotten for school, playing video games with Austin again today, and her family's plans to go to the beach tomorrow afternoon and stay until Monday. Then she responded to the things Sarah had talked about.

> *I agree with you about not dating until we're sixteen. After watching what you've been going through the past six months, I've come to the conclusion I'm not ready for dealing with boys yet either. And spending time with Austin this week has been fun—just hanging out as friends without either of us wanting anything else. I hope I can find that with other guys too instead of it always being about 'Does he like me or not, and if he does, then what?' I guess I never thought it would be so complicated.*
>
> *I will definitely be praying for you, and I love that verse you wrote at the bottom of your*

letter—the one from Psalm 91. You always find the best verses. How do you do that? Oh, yeah, you read your Bible every day. I think I need to start doing that more. I told myself I would when we got back from camp, and I did the first couple of days, but then I got lazy.

I think I'll take some time and read it right now before I go to bed. I'm always too tired in the morning. By the time you get this you'll have had your first day of school. Let me know how it goes.

Love you,
Brianne

Folding the letter and placing it into an envelope, Brianne wrote Sarah's new address on the front and laid it on her night stand, then took her Bible from the shelf to read it. She turned to Psalm 91, and she read the whole thing. It was really cool, and she highlighted a bunch of it, including verse fifteen: *When they call on me, I will answer.*

Closing her eyes for a moment, she whispered prayers for herself and for Sarah. She had prayed a lot in her life, but for the first time she had a very strong feeling God was listening and He would answer her.

In the morning she went to church as usual, but several of her friends were gone because it was Labor Day Weekend. Her family was going to the beach but not until later today. Austin played drums for the youth group. Their former drummer had graduated and left for college last week, and Austin seemed nervous about it, but he did a really good job, and she told him so when he came to sit beside her. He had been in band with her since she moved here in fifth grade, but she had never heard him play on a drum-set during church before.

"Thanks," he said, not appearing too confident in himself. "I messed up twice though."

"I didn't notice," she answered honestly.

Ashlee, Emily, and most of the junior high group was gone, so she and Austin joined in with the high school class that was smaller than usual too. Even though they were only seventh graders, the older kids knew her and Austin pretty well because their dads were the two pastors at the church.

Brianne liked the way Pastor Doug taught. She had been attending the junior high class since mid-June, and the teacher was okay, but Pastor Doug made God sound more real somehow, like her dad always did but more on her level as a twelve-year-old girl. She almost fell off her chair when he asked them to turn to Psalm 91. Numbly she turned the pages in her Bible, having the distinct feeling God was trying to tell her something. She had never read that Psalm before last night, but God had directed her attention to it again?

"As you head into a new school year, having changes to face: new classes, new teachers, new challenges, and new friends; I want you to keep in mind that God is in the details. In the ways you need to find Him, He is there. In the ways you need protection, He will provide it. In the ways you need direction, He will show you the right paths to take. Don't worry about the details; Let Him handle it. Trust Him with all of your heart, and He will be there."

Brianne realized she hadn't thought about God that way before. She had been hearing about God ever since she could remember and knew He loved her. She had asked Jesus into her heart when she was five or six. She couldn't remember an exact time, but she had always known He was there. When she was ten and understood more about what it meant that Jesus had died for her sins and risen from the dead, she had been baptized at their church in Sweet Home before they moved here.

She loved God. She liked going to church. Church was as much a part of her life as school and her family and friends, but was she letting God be a part of her everyday life? Was she looking to Him to guide her? Did she believe He really cared about her?

Ever since she heard Sarah was moving away, she had felt a little mad at God, but was it possible He could have a good reason for it and that He would provide her with a new best friend? Did He understand her fears and uncertainties about going into seventh grade, and could He give her the strength and courage to deal with it? Could she say with confidence, *'He is my God, and I am trusting Him!'*?

When Pastor Doug ended the class time with a prayer, she said her own in the quietness of her heart, asking God to help her with whatever she faced this week and in the weeks to come. She didn't know exactly what to pray for. Several things came to mind, but she decided to let God take care of her in His own way—the way that was truly best for her, not in the ways she thought would be best.

She thought Sarah should be here, but she wasn't, so she surrendered herself to God and His perfect plans, and she felt like God was right here—closer than ever before.

Chapter Five

"How are you doing, sweetheart?"

Brianne looked up from her book and saw a look in her dad's eyes that said he wasn't making casual conversation. Her brothers were making a sandcastle nearby, and her mom had taken Beth to the restroom. They had arrived at the beach about two hours ago and would be heading to dinner soon and then back to the beach house a family in the church was letting them use.

"Okay," she said, laying her book aside and tucking her knees into her chest. "I miss Sarah."

"Are you looking forward to school starting?"

"Yes."

"How do you like youth group?"

"I like it. We were in with the high schoolers today because Mark was gone, and I like the way Pastor Doug teaches. He gave me stuff to think about."

"Like what?"

"Like trusting God with the details—going back to school, making new friends, answering my dad's nosy questions," she teased.

"Speaking of nosy questions," he said. "Anything going on between you and Austin?"

"What?" she laughed, nearly choking on her sip of Dr. Pepper.

"He was at the house a lot this week."

"He was playing video games with J.T."

Her dad lifted his eyebrows. "Mom said you were playing a lot too."

She felt embarrassed and laughed. "Daddy, my best friend just moved away, I had to do something besides sit around feeling sorry for myself. Austin and I are just friends, I promise."

"Okay, just checking."

She hesitated to ask the question that entered her mind, but she took her eyes from the crashing waves and went ahead, honestly wanting to know what her dad thought. "What would you say if I told you otherwise?"

"I'd say I think you're both a little young to be going there yet."

She laughed. "I think you're right. Sarah and I decided we're not going to date until we're sixteen."

"Oh yeah?"

She smiled and he gave her a sideways hug. "I think that's a very wise decision, sweetheart."

After he released her, she asked him something on a different subject. "Why do you think God had Sarah's family move?"

He sighed. "Hard to say. I'm sure it's a lot of things—some big, some small. You'll likely never know all of them, but I think you'll see some of the reasons if you're looking for them."

"I think I may have already discovered one."

"What's that?"

"Sarah wrote me a letter, and she wrote this verse at the end of it that really encouraged me, and I realized how close to God she is. I've always known that by the way she lives and the things she says, but seeing her write out that verse made me realize I haven't been reading my Bible as much as I should. I want to, but I can never seem to stick with it. Why is that?"

"Maybe because you're not doing it to really seek God, you're just doing it."

"Where do you think I should read?"

"For your age, I think Matthew, Mark, Luke, or John would be a good place to start. Reading about Jesus, really looking at what He says: that never gets old for me. Some of Paul's shorter letters would be good too—Galatians, Philippians, Colossians; they have a lot of practical applications for everyday life. And Psalms and Proverbs do too. Or if you're more into drama, Genesis and Exodus have lots of that."

"Do you think it's okay if I read before I go to bed instead of in the morning? The speaker at camp this summer said we should always start the day with God, but I'm always so tired then."

"I think whatever works best for you is when you should. And share what you're learning with someone, like me or your mom, or in your letters to Sarah. I always get more out of it when I know I'm going to be sharing what I'm learning with someone else." He laughed. "Like every Sunday when I have to get up and tell a hundred and fifty people what God has been teaching me."

"You're still learning stuff? Daddy, you're a pastor. I thought you knew everything about God there is to know."

He laughed. "Heavens no, sweetheart. It's a lifelong journey—seeking God and getting it through our heads how much He loves us and how He works in our lives. A lot of adults think they have it all figured out, but most of us don't. God reminds me of that all the time, but He wants to show us. We just have to be willing to live and learn."

***

On Tuesday morning Brianne caught the school bus at the end of her long driveway for the first day of her seventh grade year and took an empty seat since Sarah wasn't there to sit with. The bus stopped in front of Austin's house five minutes later, and he sat beside her, which sort of surprised her, but not really. He had often sat alone in a seat near her and Sarah last year.

"How was the beach?" he asked, laying his head back against the seat like he wasn't quite awake yet. She noticed he had gotten his hair cut since Sunday.

"Good," she said. "The weather was really nice."

"Looks like you got a little sunburned."

She felt her warm cheeks. "Yes. I forgot to put sunscreen on my face. What did your family do?"

"Nothing much," he said. "Me and my dad went fishing yesterday."

"Did you catch anything?"

"I got one, and my dad got two."

"I like your shirt. Is that new?"

"My mom took me and Cal shopping after dinner last night," he said as if it was the torturing event of the century.

She laughed. "Did you pick that out, or did she?"

"I did."

"I found pink jeans at the beach yesterday. I couldn't believe it! I've been looking everywhere for a pair, and there they were at a little shop in Seaside."

"You wear a lot of pink," he commented.

"It's my favorite color. It's a happy color, don't you think?"

He turned his head and smiled at her. "A happy color?"

"Yeah, like yellow or light blue—happy colors. Not something drab like navy or green or black."

"How about red?" he asked, referring to the shirt he was wearing today.

"Red is on the edge—sort of daring. You can do your newest skateboard tricks in that shirt."

He laughed. "You're so weird."

She laughed in return. "What's your favorite color?"

"I don't know. Red, I guess."

"It's a good color for you. I see you got your hair cut."

"Shut up."

"I like it."

He was silent for a moment and then asked her something. "What's your schedule like?"

She dug the paper out of her pocket, unfolded it, and showed it to him. He took his from the front of his backpack and compared them.

"We have the same schedule," he said.

"You're kidding!" She looked over his shoulder to see the evidence for herself. They had the exact same classes and teachers at the same times all day long. She started laughing.

"That's insane," he said, handing hers back. "I'm going to be seeing pink everywhere I go."

"Sorry," she said. "I'll try and limit it to three times a week."

"No pink on Mondays," he said. "Pink and Mondays don't go together."

"Why not?"

"Because pink is a happy color, and Mondays are my least favorite days."

"Maybe a little pink will brighten your day," she said, laughing again, first at her own words and then at Austin's rolled eyes. He laid his head back again like he felt a headache coming on.

"Okay, no pink on Mondays," she said. "And no black, gray, or ugly colors for you on Fridays. Fridays are definitely pink days."

He was quiet until they reached the school. She and Sarah had always talked nonstop, but Austin was quieter, and none of his close friends rode this bus. As the bus pulled up to the school to drop them off,

Austin rolled his head to the side, opened his eyes, and spoke again.

"I'm glad, Brianne."

"Glad about what?"

"That we have all of our classes together."

"You are?"

"Sure. You're sort of the best friend I've got."

"Me? What about Michael and Jason?"

"I like hanging out with them, but we don't really talk—not about important stuff anyway."

"And we do?"

"Sure. You know, like about God and family and stuff."

"And about what girls you like?" she teased him.

"Yeah, that too."

She supposed he was right. They didn't talk like she and Sarah talked, but when they did, she always felt comfortable and like she could share what she was really thinking. They got off the bus and walked to the doors of the school. Stepping inside and heading for her assigned locker, which was in the same hallway as his, she decided to say what was on her mind.

"You know, I've been praying for a good friend to take Sarah's place." She linked her arm with his and laughed. "Maybe He's already given me one."

"Me? What about Emily?"

"I don't have classes all day with her!"

"Ashlee?"

"You give much better advice, and you don't drive me crazy after five minutes."

“Marissa?” he said, spotting her ahead of them working the combination to her locker.

“She has a lot of friends besides me.” Brianne released his arm and stepped over to her locker. “See you in five minutes?”

“Yep,” he replied.

Chapter Six

Brianne spun the locker combination on the paper in her hand and opened the metal door. Removing her pink hooded sweater she had worn to keep her warm on the ride to school, she hung it on the peg and took her notebooks out of her backpack.

"Hi, Brianne," she heard someone say.

Turning around, she saw Ashlee stepping past her, appearing as though she had just arrived. "Hi, Ash," she said. "What's your schedule like?"

Ashlee pulled hers from her backpack and handed it to her. Brianne had memorized hers enough by now to know which classes she had when.

"We have *U.S. History* and *Language Arts* together," she informed her.

"Cool," Ashlee said, taking the paper back. "What do you have first?"

"Science."

"Have fun," she said with sarcasm. The seventh grade science teacher was well known for his strict rules and eccentric personality. His real name was Mr. Thompson, but most students who didn't like him referred to him as Mr. Toadman outside of class.

Ashlee was always giving her inside information about the school and teachers because she had an older brother. Andrew was fifteen, but he wasn't a great student. He had been in trouble a lot, got poor grades, and had little respect for teachers and other authority figures—including Pastor Doug who'd had his share of trouble with him at church.

Brianne had learned to filter what Ashlee said. She had heard from other students about Mr. Thompson, but she hadn't had him herself, so she decided to wait and see what he was like, rather than setting foot in his classroom expecting the worst from him. Austin agreed with her a few minutes later.

"Ashlee can have her opinions," he said. "I prefer to form my own."

They entered the room with black lab tables and high stools to sit on. She and Austin took two seats in the second row, and Brianne hoped they wouldn't be reassigned in alphabetical order. If they were, she knew she would end up in the front, and Austin would be in the middle of the room. Having Austin for a lab partner would be nice, she thought. She knew at some point this year they would be dissecting some kind of animal, and she had been hoping for a lab partner who would be willing to do all the cutting and touching of whatever it was.

Of all her teachers, she expected Mr. Thompson to be the one most likely to assign seats, but to her surprise, he didn't. He did expect them to sit in the same place every day, but they could remain in the places they had selected for themselves today. By the end of class he had reassigned a few students to the front who had sat in the back of the classroom, but Brianne didn't blame him. One of them was Brady, who was separated from his friends and forced to sit in front of her. Brady looked less than thrilled with the arrangement, and the girl beside him looked petrified. Brianne had never seen her before and felt sorry for her having to end up with a lab partner like Brady.

Mr. Thompson didn't seem as bad as Ashlee and other students had made him out to be. He sounded strict about grades and didn't tolerate tardiness or late assignments. They would have a quiz every Wednesday and would be assigned vocabulary words every week, and he gave them homework on the first day. But Brianne had expected this year to be harder than last year. Generally if she took the time to study and do her homework, she did fine in most of her classes.

Once they were in the hallway, she asked Austin what he thought of "Mr. Toadman", and he pretty much agreed with her. "Other than reassigning Brady to sit beside that poor girl, he doesn't seem so bad."

Brianne needed to use the bathroom and told Austin she would meet him in their next class. He went on ahead, and she went into the girls' room, used the bathroom, and then saw the new girl from their science class at the sink when she went to wash her hands. Brianne decided to introduce herself.

"Hi, I'm Brianne. I was sitting behind you in science class."

The girl smiled and reached for a paper towel. "I'm Brooke."

"You're new, right?"

"Yes," she said. "I just moved here from Longview."

She needs a friend, Brianne. Be one.

Brianne smiled at her. "What class do you have next?"

"Math."

"Do you need help finding it?"

"No, it's right next door," she said. "But thanks."

They left the bathroom, and Brianne knew she needed to hurry to get to history on time, but she asked Brooke if she could see her schedule anyway. Brooke handed it to her, and Brianne smiled.

"You're in band? What instrument do you play?"

"Oboe."

"I play the flute," she said. "Do you know where the band room is?"

"No."

"You want to meet me at my locker after this class, and I'll show you?"

"Sure," Brooke said, appearing relieved. "That would be great."

Brianne quickly glanced at the rest of the schedule. "I think we have *Language Arts* together after that," she said. "And P.E. later too. Looks like we're going to be seeing a lot of each other."

Brooke smiled.

"I've gotta run," she said, handing the schedule back to her and telling Brooke her locker number. "See you."

"Okay. Bye."

Brianne hurried to her classroom and arrived just as the bell rang. Austin had saved her a seat, and she waved at Ashlee and Marissa who were also in the class but had taken seats near the back.

"What happened to you?" Austin asked.

"I met that new girl. The one sitting in front of us in science."

"Oh?"

"Yeah. Her name is Brooke. I looked at her schedule and found out we have band and some other classes together too."

Mr. Riley was ready to begin class, and their conversation ceased. The first thing Mr. Riley did was reassign them to seats in alphabetical order, so Brianne went to the front, taking the fifth seat along the front row. Austin's last name was Lockhart, so he ended up two rows back from her and on the opposite side of the room. Ashlee was a few seats over from him, and Marissa was assigned to the seat right in front of him.

Brianne felt alone for the first time today, but she supposed she had gotten off to a good start with knowing Austin would be in all of her classes. Ashlee, Marissa, and now Brooke were in a fair amount of them too. Meeting Brooke beside her locker when history was over, she took her flute case out. They began walking toward the band room, and Brianne asked her more questions.

"Why did you move here?"

"We were looking to buy a new house, and things are cheaper here than in Longview."

"Where do you live?"

"On the east end of town in those new housing developments."

Brianne knew exactly where she meant. "Those are nice," she said. "Do you like it?"

"Yes. I get my own room now instead of having to share with my sister."

"Older or younger?"

"Older. She's a sophomore this year."

"Do you have any other brothers and sisters?"

"A little brother. He's nine."

"I have three younger brothers. They're ten, eight, and eight."

"Twins?"

"No. Steven is adopted. We've had him since he was three."

"Any sisters?"

"Yes, Bethanie. She's five."

"Wow, that's a big family."

"I don't get my own room!" She laughed. "But it's okay. Beth is special. She's adopted too."

"Where do you live?"

"That way," she said, pointing west. "It's a little ways outside of town."

"How long have you lived here?"

"Almost two years."

Marissa caught up with them outside the band room, and Brianne introduced her to Brooke. Marissa greeted Brooke in a friendly way, asking if she was new and where she had moved from. They found seats in the front row. Brianne sat between Brooke and Marissa.

Miss Duncan got class started by having them warm up and then passed out music they would be required to play on Monday of next week to determine their chair placement.

It didn't look too tough to Brianne. She had been playing the flute since fifth grade, and she took private lessons too. She really loved playing and enjoyed practicing her flute more than doing any of her homework for her other classes except *Language Arts*, her favorite subject.

After band, Brianne and Brooke went to her locker so she could pick up her binder, and then they went to *Language Arts* together where Brianne introduced her to Austin. Mrs. Murphey didn't move them around but had them fill out a seating chart and expected them to sit in the same places tomorrow. Brooke was sitting beside her, and Austin had taken the seat behind her, so she was happy with that arrangement.

After class, the three of them headed for the cafeteria together, and she and Brooke sat with Austin, Jason, and Michael—one of Austin's friends Brianne hadn't seen all summer because he didn't go to church with them. She introduced Brooke to them also and then ate her peanut butter and jelly sandwich and the rest of her lunch she had brought from home, asking Brooke more questions about herself as they ate.

She found out her dad was a doctor in Longview. He had a family-practice office there. Longview was a mid-sized city in Washington State on the other side of the Columbia River from Clatskanie. Whenever her family needed to do major shopping, they usually went to Longview.

Brooke had Asian features: long silky-black hair, lightly tanned skin, and large brown eyes. Her full name was Brooke Jia Li Quan—Jia Li was after her grandmother on her dad's side.

After lunch they had a little free time before they needed to get to their next class. They both went outside and walked around for a few minutes, waiting for the bell to ring.

"Do you play sports?" Brooke asked.

"Just track," she said. "I'm not coordinated enough for anything else."

"What do you run in track?"

"Sprints. The 100, 200, and relays. I also like the long jump."

"I was in track last year, but I like distance running," Brooke said.

"Do you play any other sports?"

"I like volleyball. I was thinking of going out for the team, but I'm not sure."

"You should," Brianne encouraged her. "My friend Sarah played last year, and she really liked it."

"Have I met Sarah yet?"

"No. She moved."

"Oh," Brooke said. "How do you know Austin so well? Is he your neighbor or something? You seem like you're really good friends."

"He goes to my church. I'm the pastor's daughter, and he's the youth pastor's son, so we've gotten to know each other pretty well."

"Your dad's a pastor?"

"Yes."

"What church?"

"Rivergate Community. It's about a mile from where I live."

"We go to church in Longview," she said. "We've been thinking of finding someplace here, but we're still debating. We like it there, but it's a big church, and we were thinking something closer and smaller might be better."

Brianne was excited to hear Brooke went to church too. She could use a good Christian friend she also went to school with, especially now that Sarah had moved away. She had a thought and decided to go with it.

"We're going on a youth retreat in a couple of weeks. Would you like to come?"

"Yeah, maybe," she said. "I'll have to ask. Where are you going?"

"Camp Laughing Water. We go there in the summer for camp. It's near where I used to live in Sweet Home before we moved here."

"How far away is that?"

"About three hours. But it's worth it. It's a really nice camp—especially the retreat center. They have bathrooms with showers right in the cabins, and there's this big meeting area with a fireplace and a kitchen overlooking the lake."

"That sounds nice," she said. "I'll ask."

Chapter Seven

Dear Brianne,

I just got home from my first day at school, and it went okay. It's a pretty big school, so I think newcomers are harder to spot than they would be at Clatskanie. I sort of made a friend. Her locker is next to mine, and we have a couple of classes together. Her name is Melanie. She's on the volleyball team too, and practice was fun. Other than that, not much happened. I didn't have any guys asking me for my phone number or anything. One guy in my math class flirted with me a little and we had lunch after that, so he ended up walking me back to my locker. He was nice, but when I told him my family was looking for a good church to go to and I asked if he knew of one, he said, 'I don't go to church, but one of my friends does, so I'll ask him for you.' So we'll see if he actually does that. We visited the church our neighbors go to on Sunday. It was nice but huge! We're not sure if we want to go to a place that big, but worshiping God with about a thousand other people was pretty cool. They have youth group on Wednesday nights, so Scott and I are going to go tomorrow and check it out.

I'm glad to hear you and Austin have been spending time together. He really is a nice guy. Believe me, I've seen the difference. You could never go wrong having him for a friend, and I want you to know if he ever has feelings for you in the future that go beyond friendship, and you feel the same way about him, I would be fine with that. One of the things I've been thinking about why we had to move is I'm not sure I could have waited until we're sixteen to have him as a boyfriend if he kept asking me about it, but if he's not the right guy for me, I wouldn't want to start something that would end up being a mistake.

And along those lines, I don't think I'm going to go on the retreat this time. Maybe the next one, but I think it's better if I don't see him for awhile—give him a chance to accept the fact I'm gone rather than popping in and out of his life, you know what I mean? If you really want me to go, I will. Please be honest, Brianne. I would rather put Austin on an emotional roller-coaster than have you be mad at me. I would like to see you sometime soon though. If you want to pick a weekend to come here and visit me, I'd love that. Just let me know, and we'll work it out, okay?

I read this verse this morning and thought of you: 'I thank God for you...Night and day I constantly remember you in my prayers. I long to see you again, for I remember your tears as we parted. And I will be filled with joy when we are together again.' (2 Timothy 1:3-4)

Missing you,
Sarah

Brianne felt disappointed Sarah didn't want to go on the retreat, but she understood her reason. She had picked up the letter from the mailbox after getting off the bus and read it on the front steps with Whiskers sitting on her lap. Her older cat was usually waiting for her when she came home from school, but Molly tended to wander around in the fields surrounding their house, chasing birds and mice this time of day. Lifting her beloved cat from her legs and going inside the house, she found her mom helping Beth with an art project at the kitchen table, and she asked when she might be able to go visit Sarah.

"Whatever is good for you," she said. "I don't think we have anything major going on until that weekend conference your dad and I are going to in late October."

"Could I go on Friday and come back Sunday?"

"This Friday?"

"No, I mean whatever weekend I decide."

"Yes, that would be fine, as long as it's okay with Sarah's mom and dad."

"I'll pick a weekend and then write and see if that's okay," she said.

Beth held up a picture she had colored. "Look, Bree. I made this for you."

Brianne smiled and went to take the picture from Beth's small hands. "Thank you, sweetie," she said, giving her a hug. "I love it."

"How was school today?" her mom asked, taking the painting Beth had also made and laying it on the counter to dry.

"Okay," she said. "P.E. was tough. We had to run the mile, and they timed us. I hate having to run that far. I get a side-ache."

Her mom gave her a sympathetic look. "Sorry, baby. I'm glad those days are over for me." She laughed. "How do you like your other classes?"

"They're all right. I have a ton of homework though. I'd better get started so I can finish before I have to leave for youth group."

She went to her room, feeling excited about going to church tonight and wondering what it would be like. She had always enjoyed the midweek kids' program on Wednesday nights, but she was too old for it now and worked as a helper in the preschool room. Youth group was held on Thursdays and was for both junior high and high school students. She and Sarah had been looking forward to being able to go this year, but now she would be going without her.

Working diligently on her math and English assignments and then moving on to history, she was able to get most of it done by the time she took a break to help her mom with dinner. She finished the last of her history questions and a short science worksheet after she was done eating, and then her dad drove her to the church. She was used to getting there early for most things, but because her parents weren't in charge of anything related to youth group, she only arrived five minutes before it started, and a lot of kids were already there.

She found Emily and talked to her until Pastor Doug got their attention. Brianne enjoyed being mixed in with the high school students as they played games, sang worship songs, listened to Pastor Doug talk, and then broke into small groups to do a worksheet he had for them.

Ashlee and most of the other regulars her age were there, but something was definitely missing without Sarah. Pastor Doug encouraged them to bring friends, and Brianne thought she might invite Brooke to come over to her house after school next Thursday and then she could come to church with her too. Brooke had already decided to go on the retreat in a few weeks, and her family was planning to come to church this Sunday.

On Friday morning she boarded the bus as usual and waited for Austin to get on a few minutes later. She had enjoyed seeing him so much every day and also at youth group last night. They both fell silent after they said 'hi' to each other. Sometimes Austin listened to music on the way to and from school, and he had his earbuds in this morning.

"Can you hear me?" she asked after a minute when she thought of something to say.

He opened his eyes and rolled his head to the side. "Yep."

"I got a letter from Sarah yesterday. She had a pretty good first day at school."

He didn't respond, but he appeared to be listening.

"It doesn't seem as weird without her here as I thought it would. I thought nothing would be the same, and I couldn't even imagine her being gone, but now that it's happening, it's not so bad. I mean, I miss her, but I guess I'll survive."

He smiled. "I'm sure you will."

"Do you feel that way too, or do you really miss her a lot?"

"I never had her much to begin with."

She smiled. "Who's taking her place?"

"Huh?"

"Who do you have your eye on now instead of Sarah? I know you, Austin. Come on. Be honest."

He smiled and looked away. "Nobody."

She wasn't sure if she believed him, but she let it go.

Chapter Eight

The following Thursday, during the second week of school, a new student entered the science classroom after class had begun. Mr. Thompson looked at the slip of paper the boy handed to him, and then he assigned him to sit beside Brooke for now since Brady was absent today.

Brianne smiled at him as he took his seat, and he smiled back. He was really cute, and his smile made him even more so. Mr. Thompson was giving them a lecture about the earth's atmosphere, but she had a difficult time concentrating. The new guy was right there in her line of sight, and she couldn't seem to stop glancing at him. One time she didn't even realize she had been staring at him until he turned slightly and glanced back at her.

After that she tried to not look at him anymore, but he was still on her mind more than anything else going on around her, even when Mr. Thompson gave them the last fifteen minutes of class to study with their lab partner for their first major test tomorrow. She and Austin were studying together, but she was very much aware of the new boy quizzing Brooke from the study sheet. He would definitely make a better lab partner for Brooke than Brady, and she found herself praying Mr. Thompson would reassign Brady once again—although she was praying more for herself than for Brooke.

After class she didn't plan to go out of her way to talk to him, but Austin introduced himself, and she and Brooke stood there talking to him too. His name was Silas, making Brianne instantly wonder if he was a Christian because that was a more uncommon Bible name. He seemed nice, and she and Austin learned he had history with them next period too, so they walked with him to their classroom.

He was from California. His family had just moved here from a small town there, and Brianne wondered what had brought them to Clatskanie. Austin asked him.

"My dad is a pastor, and he just took a job here."

Austin and Brianne exchanged smiles. "Oh yeah? What church?" Austin asked.

"It's actually a new church."

"Like a church plant, you mean?"

Silas appeared surprised Austin would know what that was. "Yes. You go to church too?"

Austin laughed. "My dad is a pastor, and so is Brianne's."

Silas was walking between them, and he turned and smiled at her. "What church?"

"Rivergate Community," Austin answered. "In fact my grandpa was the one who started our church thirty years ago when my dad was just a kid. I definitely know what a church plant is."

"That's what my dad does," Silas said. "This will be the fourth one. He started two in California and one in New Mexico designed to reach American Indians, and that's what he'll be doing here too."

"Cool," Austin said. "I'm sure our dads would love to meet him. Are you Native American?"

"My dad is, but my mom isn't, so I'm half."

Brianne could see the features of his heritage now, but she wouldn't have guessed that. His hair and eyes were dark brown, but his skin was more fair. And his facial features were more European than Indian, but whatever he had gained from his parents it had all come together nicely.

By the end of the day, Austin and Silas had really hit it off. He and Brianne had two more classes with him: *Language Arts* and *Pre-Algebra,* and he also sat with them at lunch. Brianne felt sort of strange around him, like she wasn't sure how to act, but he was very nice. On the way home from school, Brianne asked Austin if he knew where Silas lived, and Austin said he hadn't thought to ask. Since he wasn't on their bus, she assumed he must live in town or on the other side, unless he was staying after school or his parents had picked him up today.

When she arrived home, the house was empty. Her mom had left a note saying she had gone to the store and would be home by three-thirty, the time her brothers arrived home from school each day. Brianne had just gotten used to being at home by herself during the last six months, and it felt strange to be all alone, but today she had a lot of homework, so she welcomed the peace and quiet and resisted the urge to turn on the television. She had youth group tonight and needed to get as much of her homework finished by then as possible. She had tests in both science and math tomorrow.

She had just finished going over her study sheet in science when the phone rang. She didn't have an extension in her room, and she went to the kitchen to answer it.

"Hi, Bree. It's me."

"Sarah?"

"Yes. Is this a good time?"

"Yeah, it's perfect. I'm the only one home right now. How are you?"

"Good. I got your email about you coming on the first weekend in October, and I wanted to let you know that's fine. Is that the weekend after the retreat?"

"Yes."

"Are you sure you're fine with me not going?"

"Yeah, I am, Sarah. Honestly. I mean, I'd love to have you there, and if you change your mind that would be okay with me, but I know what you're saying."

"Did you tell Austin I'm not going?"

"Yes. I think he's a little disappointed, but I'm sure you're right about it being better for him this way."

"How's your week going?"

"Good. Guess what?"

"What?"

"There was a new guy at school today, and Austin and I have him in four of our classes, and his dad is a pastor too."

"Oh?" Sarah laughed. "What's his name?"

"Silas. He's super nice and really cute too. And he's definitely like Austin, not Brady and Danny."

"Are you going to youth group tonight?"

"Yes, and Brooke is coming. She couldn't come over after school because she has volleyball practice, but she's going to have her mom bring her and then we'll take her home."

Sarah couldn't talk long because she had a volleyball game starting in a few minutes. She had called from school on her cell phone. When Brianne hung up, she felt really excited about going to visit her next month and in a better mood to tackle the rest of her homework.

Brianne was pleasantly surprised to see Silas at youth group that night. Apparently Austin had called him after school and invited him. During lunch Silas had told them about the churches his dad had started before. His parents were a part of a mission organization that focused specifically on reaching minority ethnic groups, mostly in rural areas. The churches tended to be small and individually designed to reach the people of that community in the best possible ways for them, so Silas and his older sister usually got connected with an established youth group in the area too.

Silas was in her small group during Bible study time, and at the end when they shared prayer requests with each other, she learned more about his sister. Danielle was fifteen, and she'd had a rough couple of years recently. Back in California she had been dating a guy who had been a really bad influence on her. She had started drinking and doing drugs and had ended up in the hospital this summer when they were in a car accident.

They were both high at the time, and her boyfriend didn't even have his license yet. He ended up in jail, and she had gotten off with probation and community service and been required to go through a rehab program, which she had done. She was drug and alcohol free now, but she still wasn't doing well emotionally and spiritually.

She didn't want to be here in Oregon, and she had already decided as soon as she turned sixteen in another few months she was going to drop out of school and get a job and move back to California where all her friends were.

Brianne could tell Silas was really concerned about her. He had a difficult time telling them about it, but he wanted them to pray for her, and he also asked for those who might see her at school to try and connect with her if they could. Those in their group who were her age said they would do that.

As everyone began to leave, Austin told Silas they had to wait for everyone else to go before they could take him home, and he said that was fine. Brianne's mom wasn't here yet, so she and Brooke sat there talking for a few minutes. She had seen Silas as being social today at school, more so than Austin, and he'd been the same way here. He didn't seem uncomfortable being around a bunch of new people, but he wasn't trying to act cool and better than everyone either.

"Where do you live, Silas?" Brianne asked.

"Right now we're staying with a family that lives near the school until we can find a place to rent."

Brianne had a strange feeling pass through her. During the past two weeks, she had been trusting God with the details of Sarah moving away and beginning her seventh grade year without her. She had seen Him answer her prayers for other good friendships and her year getting off to a good start, making her more aware of God's presence in her life and how He would take care of the details when she trusted Him to do that.

And tonight at dinner, she had whispered another prayer when her dad came home from work and told them he'd seen a "For Rent" sign on Sarah's old house. Apparently the people who bought it weren't going to be living there themselves but renting it out to someone else. When she heard that, she had prayed for good neighbors, and having Silas and his family as neighbors would definitely be an answer to that prayer.

"I know of a place," she said to Silas. "It's by my house. Right next door actually."

Chapter Nine

Silas smiled and asked for the name of the street where she lived so he could tell his mom and dad about the available house. Austin said it was on the way into town from the church, so he could point it out to him when they took him home. That strange feeling Brianne had been having around Silas hit an all-time high.

She told Silas and Austin good-bye when she saw her mom enter the parking lot from the window of the youth room. They both said they would see her tomorrow, and Austin made a special point of telling Brooke he was glad she had come tonight, which Brianne thought was sweet of him. Brooke said she wasn't sure if she could come back next week because they had a volleyball game, but she'd had fun, so Brianne was optimistic this wouldn't be the only time.

After her mom dropped Brooke off at her house, Brianne sat in the front seat of the van on the way home. Her mom asked how the night had gone, and she told her about the fun games they played and what their Bible study had been about. She hadn't said anything to her parents about Silas yet, but since he was there tonight, she went ahead and told her mom about him and his family.

"You should get his phone number tomorrow so Daddy can call them," her mom said. "I'm sure he'd love to talk to them about their ministry."

The thought of asking Silas for his phone number made her feel weird. But the following day during lunch she got up the nerve to do it, telling him what her mom had said, so it sounded like she was getting the number for her parents rather than herself. She thought he was cute and she was definitely crushing on him, but she didn't want him to know that.

He gave her the number and smiled. "I told my mom and dad about the house last night," he said. "We'll probably go see it sometime this weekend."

"It's a nice house," she said. "It's not very big, but it has a really nice yard, and the Andersons took good care of it."

"Why did they move?"

"Sarah's dad got transferred to Portland."

"Were you and Sarah good friends?"

"Best friends," Austin answered for her.

"Yes," she agreed. "I really didn't want her to move, but I guess God has His reasons. I'm going to see her next month. I can't wait."

"You are?" Austin asked. "When?"

"The weekend after the retreat. Mom and Dad are letting me go on Friday afternoon, and I'm staying the whole weekend!" she squealed. "It's going to be so fun."

"Did you ask your parents about the retreat?" Austin asked Silas, changing the subject.

"Yep. They said I can go."

Brianne was glad to see Austin and Silas becoming friends. Austin had other friends, but Brianne could see Silas and Austin becoming really good friends. And Silas wasn't just a kid who went to church but who also seemed to have a real relationship with God. He reminded her of Sarah in that respect. Austin needed someone like him as a friend, and she was glad for her sake because she had a good excuse to be around him. She felt like she could be herself with Austin and Silas together, but she wasn't sure that would be true if she had met Silas on her own.

"That would be cool if Silas lived next door to you," Austin commented on the bus ride home that afternoon.

"Yes," she said.

"You like him, don't you?"

"Sure I like him," she said.

He stared at her, and she felt the corners of her mouth turning up. "He's very nice," she tried to cover, not wanting to give her secret thoughts away.

"I've never seen you look at a guy that way, Brianne. Come on, be honest. I'm not going to say anything."

"Say anything about what? That I think he's nice?"

"It's fine if you do," he said. "He's a good guy. I'd give you permission to date him."

"*You* would give me permission? And who are you to tell me who I can and can't date?"

"Someone who cares about you a lot and would hate to see you with some loser who doesn't know how to treat you right like Silas' sister did."

She was surprised but very touched by his words. "You would?"

"Sure. Why wouldn't I?"

"I don't know. I guess I never thought about it before."

"Well, now you know."

"Thanks, Austin. That's sweet."

"Are you going to ask him to the dance?"

"What dance?"

"The one next Friday. It's girl-ask-guy, you know."

No, she didn't know that, and no, she wasn't going to be asking Silas or anyone. She had been to a couple of dances with Sarah and their friends last year, but she hadn't had a very good time.

"I've decided I'm not going to date until I'm sixteen. Sarah too."

"You're going to be breaking a lot of hearts," he said.

"I'm sure Sarah will be."

"You too."

She laughed. "Yeah right. Like who?"

"I know of at least one."

"Who, Silas?" she laughed. "Shut up!"

He didn't respond, and she changed the subject. "I asked Brooke today how she liked youth group last night, and she said she liked it."

"You two seem to be becoming good friends," he said.

"I really like her, and we get along great. Just like me and Sarah except Brooke is quieter. I hope her family starts coming to Rivergate, but they're still debating about going to a different church."

"Did you say she has a sister?"

"Yes. She's fifteen."

"I wonder if she has any classes with Danielle," he said. "Isn't she a sophomore too?"

"Yes, I think so. Had Silas mentioned Danielle before, or was that the first time you'd heard?"

"He mentioned having an older sister who was having some trouble, but he hadn't gone into details."

"How do you think that happens?"

"What?"

"A girl from a perfectly good family—a pastor's daughter getting so messed up?"

"Hard to say," he said. "My dad wonders the same thing about kids who grow up going to church, especially when they seem to be doing fine and then suddenly they're making all kinds of bad choices."

"Don't let me do that, okay? I don't want to end up that way."

"Is that official permission to tell you who you can and can't date in the future? You know, in another four years," he said as if he didn't believe she would wait that long.

"Yes, it is, Austin Lockhart. And don't let me go back on the sixteen-thing, even if you don't agree with it."

"I didn't say I don't agree with it."

"Yes, you did."

"No, I said you're going to be breaking a lot of guys' hearts."

"Are you going to hold me to it then?"

"Sure, if you want me to."

"I do. I'm serious, Austin. Sarah's gone, so I'm counting on you to be my best friend now. Tell me things even if you think I might not want to hear them."

He laughed, getting up from the seat so she could step past him to get off the bus at her stop. "Okay, but don't forget who said that."

"I won't," she said with a smile. "Bye. See you Sunday."

"Bye," he said.

She got off the bus and checked the mailbox as the bus pulled away. There was a letter from Sarah and also one from someone she had hoped to hear from but didn't know if she would: Her counselor from camp this summer. Thumper, whose real name was Megan West, was the daughter of the camp director of Camp Laughing Water. Dave and Robin West had gone to college at Seattle Pacific University with her mom and dad, and they had let her dad know about the open pastor position in Sweet Home many years ago. That was the church the Wests attended, and during the six years her family had lived there, Brianne had gotten to know the West kids really well: Megan, Jared, and Joel. Megan was five years older than her, Jared was three years older, and Joel was her age.

Megan baby-sat her and her brothers sometimes when they were younger, but when she had Megan as her counselor this summer, Megan had treated her differently. Not like a little girl but someone she was interested in getting to know for who she was now. After that week of camp, she had written Megan a letter, thanking her for being such a great counselor, and she shared what she had gotten out of her week there.

Sitting down on the front porch when she reached the house, Brianne opened Megan's letter and read the words:

Dear Brianne,

Thanks so much for writing me! I'm sorry it's taken me awhile to get back to you, but I have been thinking about you and praying. Did your friend get moved? How has it been so far without her? Is your seventh grade year getting off to a good start?

I saw your youth group is coming down to camp at the end of the month. Yea! I'd love to see you. Come up to the house when you have free time and we'll chat more. I really did like having you in my cabin, seeing you looking so grown up, and listening to you share about your life. In a way I feel like you're the little sister I never had. Little brothers aren't quite the same. Their idea of talking is answering all of my questions with one-word answers.

I do love them though. Did you ever get to see Joel that week you were here? I forgot to ask him. I know he really missed you after your family moved away. He's doing okay though. I remember Jared becoming sort of withdrawn and rebellious during his junior high years, but Joel is the same as he's always been: very sweet, easy-going, and lots of fun. And in my opinion, he's getting pretty cute too. He's going to be fighting off the girls one of these days, if he isn't already. (Don't tell him I said that. He gets embarrassed when I tease him about girls.) When you come here in a couple of weeks, you'll probably find him fishing at the lake. That's his favorite thing to do in the fall after we have the camp to ourselves again.

Anyway, I hope you write me back and let me know how things are going with you. One thing I remember about seventh grade is things that seemed so important one week were completely forgotten by the next. Don't stress, and try to enjoy it as much as possible. And remember, it's only what God thinks of you that truly matters, and He thinks the world of you! Live to please Him, no one else, and you'll be all right.

Love you,
Megan
(Thumper)

Brianne knew she would write Megan back sometime this weekend, but her thoughts turned to her younger brother Joel. She had seen him the week she was there, but only briefly. He wasn't a camper that week. He had gone on a rafting trip with his youth group, but she saw him on Friday afternoon, fishing at the lake from the dock.

Joel was one of her best friends. She had known him since she was four. He had always been in her class at the small school they attended from kindergarten to the first few months of fifth grade before she moved, and she had also seen him every Sunday at church. They played together, ran around the church, hid from their parents in one of their many secret hiding spots, been to one another's birthday parties, and spent a lot of time hiking around the camp when her family went to his house for lunch after church on Sundays.

She had missed him the most when they moved away. And yet whenever they got together, even if it was only once every six months, they were still as close as friends could be. It was never awkward or uncomfortable, just the same as it had always been.

She smiled at the thought of seeing him again soon. They had only talked briefly six weeks ago. She hoped they could have more time two weeks from today. She had missed him when they moved here, just like she was missing Sarah now; and two years later, she still did.

Chapter Ten

Brianne entered the youth room at church on Sunday morning and saw Emily sitting alone and reading a book. Emily was always reading when she wasn't busy with something else.

"What are you doing here so early?" Brianne asked, taking a seat beside her.

"My mom is singing a solo during church this morning and came early to practice."

"What are you reading?" she asked, leaning over to read the title. It appeared to be a fiction book, and Emily confirmed that by saying the name of it, who it was by, and that it was the second book in a new series she had found at the Christian bookstore yesterday.

"And you're already on the second book?"

"Sure," Emily shrugged. "I'd probably be finished with this one by now if I hadn't had a dance recital last night."

"How did it go?"

"Fine," she shrugged again.

By 'fine', Brianne knew Emily meant she had done very well, like always. Brianne had been to a few of her performances over the last two years, and Emily was by far the best dancer in her age-group and had performed with the older girls too. She was especially good at tap dancing, but her favorite was ballet.

Emily also played the flute, like herself, but she was much better and often played for church on Sunday mornings. She had been taking lessons since third grade and was a part of a community student orchestra. She also played the piano and violin.

Brianne heard voices coming down the hall, and she looked up to see Austin and Silas enter the room. They both said 'hi', and Brianne returned the greeting, feeling her heart beat a little faster at the sight of Silas. She had been wondering all morning if he would be here today.

Emily looked up from her book and appeared curious about the newcomer. Brianne introduced them. Emily said a shy hello and tucked her red hair behind her ear before going back to her reading.

The other students slowly filtered into the room over the next fifteen minutes. They sang a few songs before going to the junior high classroom where Mark, their Sunday school teacher, got class started. He handed them a worksheet, and all of them went through the Bible-reading and questions together. The lesson was on forgiveness, and most of it Brianne had heard before: 'Love your enemies; pray for them; forgive others as God has forgiven you.'

The end of the lesson focused on God's forgiveness toward people, and although Brianne had always known about the unlimited forgiveness of God that could cover all of her sins, she felt the reality of it hitting her in a deeper way. One verse in Luke 7 talked about how those who realize how much they have been forgiven by God will love Him more, and she thought about that for a moment.

Does that mean I need to do something really bad in order to love God more? That didn't make sense, and Mark said something that helped her to see the truth of it differently.

"When I was young, I used to wonder what I needed to be saved from since I was basically a good kid. But then one day my pastor talked about how knowing Jesus can not only save us from past sins, but also from future ones by helping us to never do the wrong things in the first place. None of us are good on our own. If we live a good life and avoid sin most of the time, that's not us and our own goodness and willpower, that's God helping us to make the right choices."

That made sense to Brianne, and she could see how Jesus had helped her to keep from doing some wrong things in the past, like at Ashlee's house last spring when she had been there for Ashlee's slumber party on her birthday and some of the girls had snuck out in the middle of the night to play a prank on one of Ashlee's neighbors. She'd had a really yucky feeling about it and knew they shouldn't be doing that. She hadn't participated and had remained at the house. The next day someone who had seen them called Ashlee's parents, and Ashlee got in major trouble.

Somehow her own parents had found out and asked her about it, and when she told them she hadn't been a part of it, she'd had a really good feeling she was telling the truth. Her parents had no way of knowing if she was lying to them or not, but she did, and having to lie to her parents or have them be disappointed in her definitely wasn't worth going along with her friends in doing something she knew wasn't right. At the time she had felt proud of herself, but now she knew it was really Jesus who had helped her to make the right choice.

During the prayer Mark said for all of them at the end of the hour, she felt closer to God somehow, and she thanked Him for forgiving her for the things she had done in the past that were wrong, and for helping her to make the right choices during the other times.

Help me to keep following you, Jesus. I do love you, and I want to love you more. Teach me how to do that.

On the way to the church sanctuary for the morning worship service, Brianne stopped to use the bathroom and Emily did also. While they were washing their hands, Emily asked her for more details about Silas. Brianne told her what she knew, and then Emily said she thought he was really cute, which didn't surprise her. She thought the same thing.

"He might be my new neighbor," she said as Ashlee entered the bathroom to fix her already perfect blonde hair.

"Who might be your new neighbor?" Ashlee asked.

"Silas," she said, trying to sound casual instead of as excited about the possibility as she felt. She knew Ashlee would tease her if she found out she liked him. "The people who bought Sarah's house are renting it out, and Silas' family is looking for a place. They looked at it yesterday and liked it, so they're probably going to move in there as long as someone else doesn't get it before they do."

"How do you know?"

"They stopped by our house after they were there and told us."

"He moved here this week, and you've already had him in your house? Good going, Brianne. I'm impressed. Have you asked him to the dance yet?"

"Why would I do that?"

"Well, you think he's cute, don't you?"

Brianne hesitated to answer. Ashlee was the type to blurt out that kind of information to Silas directly.

"I don't want to go to the dance," she said instead. "We're just friends, like me and Austin."

"Grow up, Brianne," she said, laughing at her as she turned away. "We're in seventh grade now. Boys are ready to be more than just friends."

Brianne didn't let Ashlee get to her. Her beautiful and outgoing friend had already had several boyfriends, starting with Brady last year. At the time Brianne had been envious of her, having such a cute boyfriend and being so beautiful too, but since she had learned what Brady and other guys could be like from Sarah, she had stopped envying Ashlee whenever she saw her holding hands or whatever with a boy at school. She still envied her perfect hair and cute clothes sometimes, but she was trying not to.

The following day at lunch Ashlee came over to the table where she and Brooke were sitting with Austin and Silas and some others, and she asked Silas if she could talk to him for a minute. They went into the hallway but weren't gone long.

"What was that about?" Austin asked after Silas returned.

"She asked me to the dance on Friday," he said.

"What did you say?"

"I told her no. I don't want to go with anyone."

Austin seemed impressed, and Brianne definitely was. Guys didn't turn down Ashlee Moore, at least not any she'd ever heard of.

When she stopped by the bathroom on the way to math class, Ashlee was there, sitting against the wall and crying her eyes out.

"He's a jerk," one of her friends said. "Forget about it, Ash. Ask Brady. He told me he would go with you if you ask him."

Ashlee noticed her then and spoke in her usual dramatic way. "Stay away from him, Brianne. He's not as sweet as you think."

"Who?"

"Silas. He said no when I asked him to go to the dance with me!"

Brianne held back a smile. "Maybe he doesn't want to go with anybody."

"No. He wants to go with someone, it's just not me, but he didn't have the guts to tell me that."

"How do you know he wants to go with someone?"

"All guys want to go with someone."

"Austin doesn't."

"That's because he's in love with his precious Sarah. If she was still here, he would want to go with her."

Brianne supposed that was true, but Silas had only been a student here for three days. She didn't respond further, and while she was using the bathroom, Ashlee and her friends left.

Brianne didn't give any of it much thought until the following day. After band she and Brooke walked back to the main hallway to drop their instruments back in their lockers and get their binders. They met up with Silas on their way to class as usual, but Brianne got a strange feeling when Silas said 'hi' to her. She had seen him in history an hour ago, but he acted like he hadn't seen her all day, and he kept glancing at her and smiling all the way there.

Leaving the room with her friends forty-five minutes later, feeling hungry and ready for lunch, Brianne was thinking more about the assignment Mrs. Murphey had given them than the strange way Silas had been looking at her earlier. They were supposed to write a short story, and she thought that would be fun, but she wasn't sure what she would write about.

She couldn't ignore the smile on Silas' face when she noticed him looking at her again. Returning his smile this time, she laughed and had to say something.

"What?" she asked.

He stopped walking, and she did too. Their other friends didn't notice and kept walking, leaving them alone together in the crowded hallway.

"I'd love to, Brianne," he said. "I'm glad you didn't believe what I said yesterday about not wanting to go with anyone."

She had no idea what he was talking about. "Go where?"

He laughed. "Did you forget already?"

"Forget what?"

He got a confused expression on his face. Pulling a folded note out of his pocket, he held it up. "This. The note you left in my locker, asking me if I'd go to the dance with you?"

"What?" she laughed. "I didn't leave you a note."

He raised his eyebrows and unfolded the piece of notebook paper, holding it out for her to see. It had hearts all over it and smelled like sweet perfume. She looked at the words and felt her heart start pounding so hard it hurt.

Dear Silas,

I really like you and think you're super-cute. Will you go to the dance with me?

Love, Brianne

Chapter Eleven

Brianne stared at the note, having no idea what to say. She recognized Ashlee's handwriting, and she felt incredibly mad at her, sorry for Silas, and totally embarrassed for herself. Yes, she liked Silas and thought he was "super-cute", but she didn't want him to know that. She felt like crying.

"I'm sorry," she said, looking up at him. "I didn't write this."

"You didn't?"

She shook her head and swallowed hard. "No. That's not my handwriting."

"Oh," he said, appearing disappointed. "So you don't want to go to the dance with me?"

How am I supposed to answer that? In a way I do, but I don't think I'm ready for this.

"I don't want to go with anyone," she said. "I wasn't even planning to go."

"Who wrote this?" he asked. "Do you know?"

"Someone you turned down yesterday."

"Ashlee?"

She nodded.

"Why would she do that?"

"I have no idea. I'm sorry, Silas."

He didn't respond, and she thought of something but wasn't sure if she should ask him the question on her mind. He had told Ashlee he didn't want to go with anyone, but he was accepting her phony invitation. He turned away and began walking before she could decide what else to say. She felt awful.

Why didn't I say I'd go? Maybe Ashlee's right about boys not wanting to just be friends. Maybe he thinks I've been flirting with him all this time, and now I hurt his feelings and he's never going to speak to me again. Oh, Jesus. What am I supposed to do? Why can't Sarah still be here? She would know what to do. Why did you have to take her away?

She didn't let Silas get too far before catching up to fall in step beside him. She didn't say anything and knew he felt embarrassed. She wanted to tell him she did like him and would love to go to the dance with him, which was true in a way, but she didn't want to change things between them—not yet. Sarah was definitely right about this boy-stuff being complicated.

Silas' locker was in a different hallway than hers, so when they separated, she simply said she would see him in a few minutes at lunch, but by the time she had reached her locker and pulled her lunch from the top shelf, she decided to go find Ashlee. She couldn't believe she had done such a thing. That was really low—even for her. And why had she? As a joke? It made no sense to her.

She found her in the cafeteria waiting in line for hot lunch. "Ashlee, why did you put that note in Silas' locker?" she demanded in a loud whisper.

Ashlee turned and didn't try to play innocent. "To see what he would say."

"Why?"

"What did he say, Brianne?"

"He said he wanted to go with me."

"Just what I thought," Ashlee said, sounding very satisfied with herself. "He's a liar."

Brianne took a moment for Ashlee's words to sink in. "That's why you did it, to see if he was lying to you about not wanting to go with anyone?"

"Yep. And I was right. Nobody lies to me and gets away with it."

"But you wrote a note and signed my name without asking me permission. And you think that's okay? Why did you have to pull me into this?"

"Because I knew you were the one he wanted to go with instead of me."

"How did you know that?"

"I just did," she shrugged. "What are you so mad about? You should be thanking me."

"Thanking you?"

"Sure. Now you have a date for the dance."

"I'm not going," she said.

"Why not? You like him, don't you?"

"I don't want to go to dances with guys yet."

"Oh, please, Brianne. You would rather go with Austin, is that it?"

Brianne turned away and felt incredibly angry, angrier than she had ever felt about anything. Carrying her lunch and going out the side door, she was about to sit at an unoccupied table and eat by herself in the courtyard when she felt someone grab her arm.

"Hey, what's up with you?"

She turned to face Austin and burst into tears. He pulled her against him and let her cry. By the words he spoke, she knew Silas must not have told him about the note.

"Okay, what did Ashlee do this time?"

"Silas didn't tell you?"

"Silas didn't tell me what?"

She sat down with a sigh and told Austin everything. "I know Ashlee isn't the best friend I've ever had, but I can't believe she would do something like that. And she's not even sorry. She thinks she did me a favor!"

"Are you sure she didn't?"

"What? Of course not! How can you even say that, Austin Lockhart?"

"Whoa," he laughed, holding up his hands. "I'm sorry. I shouldn't have said that."

"Then why did you?"

"Because I think you like Silas more than you're admitting to yourself."

"I do like Silas! I just don't want to go to the dance with him or anyone. I'm not ready for that. Why doesn't anyone believe me? Because I'm in seventh grade and I think some guy is cute and nice? That doesn't mean I have to start being his girlfriend, does it? I think you're cute and nice, but we're just friends. Why can't I have that with Silas too?"

Austin smiled at her. "You think I'm cute?"

"Shut up," she sulked, turning away from him. "Just go away and leave me alone."

He put his chin on her shoulder and whispered to her from behind. "I'm sorry," he said. "You're right. It can be however you want it to be, and Ashlee had no right to do what she did."

She felt like crying again, but she held back the tears this time. Crying wasn't going to solve anything.

"What am I supposed to do, Aus? I don't want Silas to think I don't like him, because I do. And he might be my new neighbor. I don't want things to be weird between us."

"Just talk to him and be as honest as possible."

She sighed and felt the anger for Ashlee returning. Why did she have to complicate her life like this? *Why am I even friends with her?*

"Come inside and eat with us," Austin said, rising from the bench and pulling her with him. "Sitting out here by yourself isn't helping anything."

She went with him, knowing he was right, but at the same time not wanting to. Taking the seat beside Brooke and across from Austin as usual, she glanced at Silas and gave him a little smile. He still seemed embarrassed, but he smiled back. Brooke didn't ask her what was wrong, for which she was grateful. She ate her lunch, and the four of them sat mostly in silence, listening in on conversations going on around them more than having their own.

By the time she was finished eating, she knew she needed to talk to Silas again, but she didn't want to.

She wasn't used to talking to boys in that way, and the fact she really did like him made it more complicated.

She ended up leaving with Brooke when she said she needed to get something out of her locker—notes she wanted to look over before her history quiz she had next period. On the way there, Brooke asked her what was wrong, and she told her.

"I thought you and Ashlee were friends?"

"We are, but I'm not sure why. She's always doing stuff I can never imagine her doing until she does. When will I ever learn?"

"Don't blame yourself, Brianne. She's the one who hurt Silas, not you."

"I know, but I hate that she hurt him. I feel terrible. Maybe I should write him another note and tell him I'd like to go but I was so shocked before, I didn't know what to say."

"Do you though? Telling him another lie doesn't seem right."

"Yeah, I know," she said. "But maybe I should want to go with him. What's stopping me? He's nice and cute, and he wants to go with me."

"But you'll have to convince him you really do want to go, and if you don't, he'll know. It's probably better to leave it alone, unless you're ready to be his girlfriend. Are you?"

She wanted to say yes, but she knew she wasn't. "No," she said. "But I don't want to lose him as a friend either."

"I don't think that will happen. You're not like Ashlee, and he knows that. Just give it a day and see what happens."

Brooke's words reminded her of the ones Megan had written in her letter about things that seem so huge one week being forgotten by the next, but she didn't know if that was possible this time.

She saw Silas again in math class, and they both took their normal seats, but his was in the back so she couldn't look at him without turning all the way around, and she had no idea if he was watching her and still thinking about it, or if he had totally forgotten by now.

She didn't get a chance to talk to him after class either, and she didn't usually see him after that because he didn't have P.E. with her and Austin, and his mom picked him up after school, but when she returned to her locker to collect her things before heading for the bus, he was there waiting for her.

"Hi," she said, feeling happy to see him and awkward at the same time.

"Hey," he said, sounding concerned for her. "Are you all right?"

She unzipped her backpack and began putting the books into it she would need tonight. "Sure," she sighed.

"If you want me to go away, just say so."

She stopped her packing and looked at him. "I'm not mad at you, Silas. I'm mad at Ashlee."

He didn't say anything else. She zipped up her bag and put her pink sweater over her shirt. Taking her flute and music, she tucked the folder in the front pouch and set her flute beside her backpack before closing the locker and turning to face him.

"I'm embarrassed," she said, deciding to be completely honest. "I'm embarrassed because I really do like you, and if I was going to go to the dance with anyone I would want it to be with you."

"But?"

"But I'm not ready to be more than friends with boys yet. I do think you're nice and cute like Ashlee wrote in the note, and I don't want you to think otherwise, but I don't want to be your girlfriend or whatever either."

"I feel the same way, Brianne."

She stared at him for a moment. "But you—"

"But I what? Accepted the invitation of a pretty girl to a dance?" he said, letting his adorable smile emerge. "I'm not sure I'm ready for that either, but when I read the note, I felt like I couldn't turn you down for the world."

She returned his smile. "But you turned down Ashlee."

"Austin had already warned me about Ashlee, and I'd seen enough for myself to know I didn't want to go with her anyway."

"But you would want to go with me if I asked for real?"

"Yes."

She picked up her backpack and slung it over her shoulder, realizing both Sarah and Austin had been right about boys beginning to notice her too. And she felt surprised and blessed her first admirer would be someone like Silas. He was definitely one of the good ones.

"I need to go or I'm going to miss the bus," she said, deciding to believe Silas was being honest with her but she didn't have to try and fix this by going against what she wanted.

He walked beside her to the doors where the busses were waiting outside. Before she stepped out, he told her not to worry about the note and he was fine with them just being friends.

"For now, anyway," he said with a smile. "I think you're nice and super-cute too, Brianne."

She heard the teasing in his voice and knew this unbelievable and crazy day was coming to an official end. Tomorrow they could go back to the way it had been before—maybe not exactly, but for now they had an understanding.

"Bye," she said, giving him a friendly smile. "Thanks for talking."

"See you tomorrow."

She turned away and hurried toward the bus, finding it nearly full. Slipping into the seat beside Austin, she let out a sigh and closed her eyes.

"Did you talk to Silas?"

"Yes. Did you tell him to talk to me?"

"He asked me if I thought he should."

"Thanks," she said. "I feel better now."

"What did you tell him?"

She laughed. "None of your business."

"Are you going to the dance with him?"

"No."

"Are you going to the dance at all?"

"I don't know," she said in a whiny voice. "Why do we have to grow up, Austin? This is getting too complicated."

"It's just a dance, Brianne. You can go and have fun."

She thought for a moment. She had gone to dances in the past to have fun, but it never seemed to turn out that way. She would end up mad at her friends who danced with boys more than talking with her, and mad at the guys who didn't ask her to dance.

But even if things might be different this time, she didn't feel right about going. She would rather do something like have a bunch of friends over to her house to watch a movie or something, except her house wasn't very big.

"I don't think so," she said to Austin, going with her gut-feeling for now. "Maybe next time."

Chapter Twelve

"How was school today?"

Brianne let her backpack fall to the floor with a thud and answered her mom's question.

"Awful," she said, plopping into a dining room chair and laying her forehead on her folded arms. She'd had a chance to talk to Silas and felt better about the whole thing, but she still wished she could start this day over and stop Ashlee from writing that note.

"What happened?" her mom asked, sounding concerned but not too alarmed.

"Ashlee embarrassed me—really bad this time. I hate her!"

"What did she do?"

"Bree, I made this for you," she heard Beth say, coming into the room and wanting to show her something she had made today either at kindergarten this morning or here at home this afternoon.

Brianne broke out of her troubled thoughts, lifting her head and taking the flimsy picture frame from her sweet little sister. She had made it out of paper and tape and put a picture of herself in it.

"Thank you," she said, lifting Beth onto her lap. "I love it."

"I made it," she repeated.

"I know you did, and you did a very nice job."

"That's a picture of me," she giggled. "Mama gave it to me."

Brianne gave Beth a gentle squeeze, wishing she could stay home all day with her instead of having to go to school. Sometimes she wished she was homeschooled like Emily, and this was one of those times.

The phone rang, and her mom picked it up. Brianne's heart leapt when she heard her mom respond to the caller.

"Hi, Sarah. How are you?"

Brianne set Beth down gently but then sprang out of the chair, silently demanding the phone from her mom.

"Okay. I think she's anxious to talk to you today."

Brianne took the phone from her mom and walked into the other room. "You'll never guess what Ashlee did to me today!"

"What?"

"She put a note in Silas' locker saying she liked him and thought he was super-cute and wanted to go to the dance with him, but she signed my name instead of hers."

"Who's Silas?"

"The new guy I told you about last week."

"Oh, yeah. I forgot," she said. "Why did Ashlee do that?"

Brianne told her the whole story, from Ashlee asking Silas to the dance yesterday, to talking to her today at lunch and asking why she had put the note in his locker.

"I can't believe she did that just because he turned her down. How could she drag me into it?"

"Who knows?" Sarah said. "It's Ashlee, Bree. I never get half of what she does."

"I hate her!" she fumed. "Why couldn't she have moved away instead of you?"

"Don't do that, Bree," Sarah said.

"Do what?"

"Hate Ashlee."

"Why not? Wouldn't you?"

"You have every right to be angry, Brianne, and I'm mad she did that to you, but you have to forgive her and let it go."

Brianne didn't want to, and she began to feel angry at Sarah too. *That's easy for you to say since it didn't happen to you!*

"I know you don't think you should have to do that. I didn't either when Brady told everyone we were going out and he kept bugging me after I told him to leave me alone, but I did, and I felt a lot better after that. And when he talked to me, it didn't bother me so much."

"So you're saying I need to forgive Ashlee for me?"

"Yes. Being angry at her will hurt you much more than it will ever hurt her."

Brianne didn't respond further. She suddenly wondered why Sarah had been calling her, but Sarah said something else before she could ask.

"Did you talk to Silas at all after that?"

"Yes. He was really sweet about it, and I felt better after I was completely honest with him."

"What's that mean?"

"I told him I'm not ready to be more than friends with boys yet, but I do like him, and that if I was going to the dance with anyone, I would want it to be with him."

"You're kidding me!" Sarah gasped. "You told him that?"

"Yes. Is that bad?"

"No. It's great. I'm so proud of you."

Brianne felt a little better.

"I have some good news. Do you want to hear it?"

"Yes."

"I've decided to go on the retreat after all."

"You are! That's great!"

"I thought about it and decided I can't avoid Austin or other guys because of how they might be feeling about me. I need to be myself and let God handle them. I really do want to see you and everyone, and I could use a weekend with friends I know well. With so many people at this school, you would think I'd have tons of new friends by now, but it's hard to connect with anyone. Everyone's really busy, and those I have gotten to know already have other friends."

"Oh, Sarah. I'm so glad. I can't wait!"

"I know. Me too. I decided last night after talking to my mom about it, and I couldn't wait to tell you."

"Do you have another volleyball game today?"

"Yes. I need to go."

"Okay, thanks for talking, and I'm sooo excited you're going with us!"

"I'll call you next week and we'll work out the details."

"Okay, bye."

"Bye. Love you."

Brianne clicked off the phone and went to share the happy news with her mom.

"That's great, honey," she said. "Does that make up for the rest of your day?"

She laughed. "Yeah, I guess."

"So what happened with Ashlee?"

Brianne sat down and told her mom the whole story too, feeling a little embarrassed to admit her true feelings about Silas, but her mom didn't seem surprised or disapprove in any way.

"Sarah said I need to forgive her. I suppose she's right, huh?"

"Yes. What she did was terrible—to you and to Silas, but your anger will hurt you much more than it will ever hurt her."

Brianne needed to get started on homework, so she went to her room, but before she got out her textbooks, she took her Bible from her night stand and opened to where her paper from Sunday was still in its place. She looked at the top of the page where several verses were listed and saw she had left the paper on the same page as one of them in Ephesians Four. Verses 31 and 32 said, *Get rid of all bitterness, rage, anger, harsh words, and slander, as well as all types of malicious behavior. Instead, be kind to each other, tenderhearted, forgiving one another, just as God through Christ has forgiven you.*

"Well, God," she whispered, "Ashlee certainly didn't act tenderhearted and kind to me or Silas today, and I am angry at her, but I know I have to forgive her and so I do. But it's going to be hard for me to be around her. Help me to show her love I don't feel right now, and also help me to be myself around Silas."

She smiled at the thought of him. Maybe Ashlee had done her a bit of a favor today. She wasn't going to admit that to anyone else, especially Ashlee, but she thought again of how sweet Silas had been the two times he talked to her, and the reality sunk in a little more that he actually liked her in that way—that he would say yes if she asked him to the dance for real!

After getting some of her homework done, she went to the kitchen to help her mom with dinner, and she decided to ask about the possibility of inviting some friends over on Friday. At first she had dismissed the idea because she didn't think any of them would choose coming to her house over going to the dance, but then she remembered Emily wouldn't be going because she didn't go to her school, and Brooke said she might go but didn't sound too set on it. If they were the only ones who came, that would be fine, and they could turn it into a sleepover.

"Do you think it's weird I don't want to go to the dance?" she asked after putting the wrapped French bread into the warm oven. "Especially since there's a boy I know would go with me?"

"I think it's honest, Brianne. I know I used to go to a lot of dances when I was your age, and I didn't really enjoy them. I finally stopped during my freshman year of high school, and I never missed them. I went to one formal dance my senior year, and that was okay because I went with a good friend."

"Who did you like in seventh grade, Mom?"

"Hmmm, seventh grade," she said, taking a moment to think while breaking the spaghetti noodles and dropping them into the pot of water on the stove. "Let's see, that would have been Brad Richardson. Me and half of the girls in my class, but I was certain he was going to notice me one day."

"Did he?"

"Not really," she laughed. "My friend Tracy, but not me."

"How old were you when you went on your first date?"

"I met a couple of different boys at the movies a few times my sophomore year, although it was more like my friend Denise was going to be meeting someone and she would have her date invite someone for me too, but that was my first time really spending time with boys like that. But my first real date was when I was seventeen."

"Who was it with?"

"His name was John, and he was the pastor's son at our church. We went out for pizza and then to a concert, and it was a good first date, actually. He was very nice."

"Did you go out with him again after that?"

"We spent time together at church and on youth activities, but we never became more than friends."

"Did he ever kiss you?"

"No," she said, reaching for the spoon and stirring the spaghetti sauce.

Her mom said that with a certain smile on her face, and Brianne had to ask what that was for.

"The first guy I ever kissed was your dad."

"He was?"

"Yes."

"But you didn't know him until you were twenty."

"That's true. I was waiting for the right one to give me my first kiss."

"How long did you make Dad wait?"

She laughed. "Not long."

"How long?"

"Let's see, I met him on the first day of my third year of college, which would have been a Monday, he asked me out on Thursday, and on Saturday night we went to see a movie, got pizza afterwards, and stayed there talking for about two hours, and then he drove me back to my dorm and kissed me at the door before I went inside."

"Mom! You waited all that time and then kissed him on the first date?"

She laughed. "Oh yes. I did."

"How did you know he was the right one?"

"I just did. I felt something in my heart I'd never felt before: something beyond attraction and curiosity. Something I knew I'd been waiting for."

Brianne smiled and thought about her mother's words several times that evening. She hadn't imagined being kissed by a boy yet, and she wasn't sure how she felt about the idea of Silas or any boy kissing her. She wondered if she would marry one of the boys she knew now—being friends with him for the next few years, dating him at some point in high school, and then marrying him sometime after that, or if she hadn't met him yet.

After getting into her pajamas, she read her Bible as she had gotten into the habit of doing before bed, and then she whispered some prayers about facing Ashlee and Silas tomorrow and about inviting friends over on Friday. Turning out her light and lying there for a few minutes, she asked God for one more thing: *Help me to wait for the right boys to date and to kiss, and help me to be myself with whomever I'm with, whether we're just friends or something more.*

Chapter Thirteen

On Wednesday morning Brianne decided not to say anything to Austin about her plans for Friday until she had a chance to ask Brooke and Emily if they could come. If both of them could, then she would invite Austin and Silas and some other friends, and if none of them wanted to, then it could just be her and Emily and Brooke having a sleepover.

Brooke didn't hesitate to say yes, and she sounded relieved she wasn't planning to go to the dance either. She called Emily after she got home from school, and Emily said she could come too, but she wouldn't be able to stay overnight because she had a private dance lesson at nine o'clock on Saturday morning. It was just as well because much to Brianne's surprise, several others, including Austin and Silas, accepted her invitation when she passed around simple fliers to the other seventh graders at youth group.

"What about the dance?" Ashlee said. "Why are you having it on the same night?"

"Because not everyone wants to go."

"That's stupid, Brianne. There's nothing wrong with going to a dance."

"I didn't say there was anything wrong with it. I just don't want to, and I thought maybe I wasn't the only one."

Ashlee obviously didn't agree, but she let it go until Friday morning after history class. "I hope you and your little friends have fun at your party tonight, Brianne."

Brianne tried to ignore her and continue to have a forgiving spirit, but it wasn't easy.

"What was that about?" Marissa asked on the way to the band room.

"I'm having friends over to my house tonight instead of going to the dance. Ashlee thinks it's stupid."

"Dances can be stupid too. Actually, I don't think it's the dances, it's the stupid boys at the dances."

Brianne laughed. "Are you going, or would you like to come to my 'little party'?"

"Sure, I'd love to. What time is it?"

"Six. We're going to be having pizza and lots of snacks, so don't eat before you come."

"Okay."

When everyone arrived, they ate first and then the guys played video games with her brothers while she and the other girls went to her room and listened to music while painting their nails and talking. Brianne got out her latest scrapbook she had been working on. It was mostly filled with pictures from the summer, and Marissa flipped through it while sitting on her bed. Marissa didn't know the other girls too well, but she asked how Sarah was doing, and Brianne told her things she knew Sarah wouldn't mind her sharing.

Both Emily and Brooke were going on the retreat next weekend, and they were excited about it. "Do you think you'll get to see Joel this time?" Emily asked, looking up from where she was painting Beth's tiny nails bright pink.

"I think so," she said.

"Who's Joel?" Marissa asked.

Brianne was about to answer when Emily interrupted her. "Joel—" she said, stretching out his name dramatically, "is the guy Brianne wants to marry."

Brianne laughed and swatted her arm. "He is not! I said that when I was in third grade."

"I'll marry him if you don't want to," she said.

"You've only met him once."

"So? Has he gotten ugly since then?"

"Who is he?" Brooke asked this time, flapping her hands in the air to dry her purple nails.

"He lives at the camp we're going to for the retreat. It's close to where I used to live. We went to church and school together up until fifth grade when I moved here."

"And she misses him desperately," Emily added.

"I do not," she laughed, taking Beth into her arms when she came over to sit with her.

"You were disappointed when you couldn't see him more this summer."

"So? I hadn't seen him since New Year's. He's one of my best friends."

"Do I get to meet him next weekend?" Brooke asked.

"Sure, if you want. I'll probably try and find him on Saturday."

"Find him?"

"He might be at his house or he might be fishing or something. It's a big camp. There are lots of places he could be besides at home."

Emily tattled on her again. "They went for a walk one day during the week we were at camp last summer," she teased.

"It was a hike," Brianne said, wondering why she was being so defensive. "He had found an eagle's nest, and he wanted to show me."

"What is it with you and boys?" Brooke asked. "You're good friends with like six of them, but you don't even play video games or go to the skate park."

"Six?"

Brooke said the names of those who were here tonight plus some from school. "Austin, Silas, Tim, Jason, Michael, and now I hear about Joel?"

"So, I have guys as friends. What's wrong with that?"

"Nothing. I'm just wondering."

"I guess I never really thought about it. Before Sarah moved I didn't spend much time with them, except for Joel. You spend as much time with those guys as I do."

"I know, but I just sit there. You talk to them."

"I've known them longer."

"No, there's something about you, the way you talk to them. It's natural and easy. I think it's great. I wish I could do that."

"She's right," Marissa chimed in. "Most of the guys I hang out with end up being jerks, but you know some good ones."

"I'm just being myself," she said with a shrug.

At seven-thirty they put in a movie and ate snacks. It was one most of them had seen, but it was a good one, and Brianne enjoyed watching it in her small living room with all of her friends.

When the movie ended, her dad turned it off and made a joke about it being time for the sermon before they were free to go home. Her friends who lived close by called their parents to have them pick them up, and those who lived farther away, her dad said he would take home.

"This was cool, Brianne," Austin said, standing out on the porch with her and waiting for his dad. "Maybe next time I'll have something like this at my house."

"You think it was better than going to the dance?"

"Without Sarah there? Sure."

She laughed and decided it was the perfect time to tell him Sarah's change of plans. "She's coming next weekend."

"Since when?"

"Since I talked to her on Tuesday."

"And you're just now telling me?"

"I had other things on my mind with the whole Ashlee and Silas thing."

"You seem okay with all of that. Are you?"

"Yes. Silas has been really great about it, and Ashlee—well, I've forgiven her, but she's not exactly on my best-friend list right now."

"Is that why you didn't invite her tonight?"

"I invited her. She just didn't come. She asked Brady to the dance."

"I'm not sure who I feel sorrier for."

"You're bad," she laughed and then spoke seriously. "I'd really hate to see her get back together with him."

"Yeah, that's probably not good."

Brianne was surprised at the genuine concern she felt for her. Ashlee hadn't been the best friend to her in the past, even before what happened this week, and yet she still cared about her.

On Sunday morning after church when she was hanging out with her friends who were waiting for their parents to get done talking, she asked Ashlee how the dance had been.

"Okay," she said, not sounding too thrilled.

"Are you and Brady back together?"

"Not really. He was kind of a jerk at the dance."

"What did he do?"

"Danced with Caitlin more than me."

Brianne didn't comment. Caitlin and Brady had been an item on and off since Ashlee had broken up with him last year. And Caitlin had been one of Ashlee's best friends before that. It was all too much drama for her to keep up with.

"Personally, I think you deserve better," she said.

"You're a bad liar, Brianne."

"I'm not lying."

"Whatever," she said.

Why do I even bother?

"Hey, Brianne," she heard someone say behind her. She turned and saw Silas. He usually went home with Austin after church.

"Hey," she said.

"Guess what?"

"What?"

"We got the house."

"You did?"

"We're going to be neighbors."

She laughed. "That's so cool!"

He smiled. "Once we get moved in, I'll have you over sometime so you can meet Danielle, okay? I can't get her to come here, but she can't keep me from inviting my friends over to the house."

"I'd like that," she said, not really knowing what she might say to her or why Silas wanted them to meet, but she would accept the invitation when it came.

Chapter Fourteen

Brianne came down with a mild cold on Monday afternoon, and she stayed home from school on Tuesday. She hoped she would be over it by the weekend. She didn't want to miss the retreat or feel miserable while she was there. She almost stayed home on Wednesday, but she had two tests, so she went, thinking she might have her mom pick her up at lunch because both of her exams were before that, but she felt okay and decided to stick it out for two more hours.

During math she had to go to the restroom to get more tissue because there wasn't any in the classroom. On her way there she saw Marissa, and it looked like she was leaving school early. She asked, and Marissa said she had to go, but she didn't explain why.

On Thursday when they sat down to start warming up in band, she remembered and asked Marissa if everything was all right. She had seemed a little upset yesterday when she was leaving and still seemed sad today.

"My mom is in the hospital."

"Why?"

"Promise you won't tell anyone?"

"Yes."

"She has Bulimia. It's an eating disorder she falls into once in awhile. Yesterday she collapsed at work, and they had to call an ambulance. That's why I left school early."

"I'm sorry," Brianne said. "Is she okay?"

"She'll come home today hopefully, but it will take awhile for her to be herself and start eating right again."

Brianne didn't know what to say, and she felt surprised Marissa would tell her because they weren't super-close friends, but Marissa's next words made more sense.

"Do you think maybe you or your dad could pray for her? She's been to so many doctors and counselors, but it's like no one can help her."

"Yeah, we can do that," she said.

"Thanks. It's just so hard. I don't even want to go home tonight."

Marissa started to cry, and she excused herself before anyone else noticed. She was gone for five minutes and then returned. Brianne didn't say anything about it until after class, but she had thought of something and decided to offer Marissa an option besides going home. She knew Marissa had a volleyball game after school today along with Brooke. Brianne had already planned on staying to watch Brooke play. Her dad was picking them both up and then Brooke was going home with her because they had youth group tonight.

She told Marissa that and then said, "If you want, you could come over too, unless you need to be at home."

"Not really," she said. "I'm supposed to call my dad when it's over."

"If it's all right with him, it's all right with me. You could have dinner with my family and go to church with us tonight."

"Thanks," she said. "I might do that. I'll call him after school and see if it's okay."

It turned out to be fine with her dad because her mom needed to stay at the hospital another night, so after the game both Marissa and Brooke went to her house where they got their homework done and ate dinner before leaving for youth group. It was a fun night, but Marissa seemed to like the worship time the most. Brianne knew Marissa didn't attend church regularly, but she didn't know what Marissa knew or believed about God. Apparently she believed in Him because she had asked her to pray for her mom, but she didn't know how much she believed in God's ability or willingness to answer.

Brianne had told Marissa it was okay if she spent the night too, and Marissa thought she might, but after they dropped off Brooke at her house, she said she felt better and wanted to hear how her mom was doing, so they took her home.

When Brianne got out of the van with her, Marissa gave her a hug in the driveway. "Thanks, Brianne. I don't care what Ashlee says about you, I think you're the nicest person I've ever known."

"Thanks," she laughed. "I think."

"Don't worry, I don't listen to Ashlee much. What was she talking about tonight with not going on that thing this weekend just because it's at the camp you went to this summer?"

Brianne shrugged. "I don't know. It's a great camp. I'd go there every month if I could."

"Is it for anyone, or just those who go to your church all the time?"

"It's for anyone. Do you want to come?"

"Can I? Once my mom comes home it will be stressful for a few days. I feel like I need to get away this weekend, and it sounds fun."

"Sure, if you want. Sarah's going to be there."

"I'll ask my dad," she said. "When are you leaving?"

"Tomorrow at four-thirty, and we're meeting at the school because a bunch of students will have to leave from there."

"Okay, I'll let you know. What do I need to bring?"

"A sleeping bag, pillow, warm clothes for the evenings—It's in the mountains."

"Am I supposed to pay anything?"

Brianne knew they were supposed to, but she also knew the church helped those who couldn't afford it, and she didn't want the money to stop Marissa from going, so she said, "No, don't worry about it. I'll talk to Pastor Doug."

"Okay, see you tomorrow," she said, giving her another quick hug. "Bye."

"Bye," she echoed and got into the front seat of the van. She hadn't had a chance to talk to her dad yet about Marissa's mom, so she did on the way home and also about her wanting to go on the retreat. "I hope that's okay," she said. "I know we were supposed to be signed up by last Sunday."

"I'm sure it's fine, sweetheart. Pastor Doug always welcomes more."

In the morning she told Austin about Marissa maybe going. He wondered why she had been at youth group last night, and Brianne said she had stuff going on at home.

"How is Sarah getting there?"

Brianne smiled. "I've missed that."

"What?"

"Being your little informant on Sarah's latest thoughts and actions."

He smiled and didn't deny it.

"She's getting out of school at noon, and her mom is driving her here."

"Do you think she would be annoyed if I tried to sit by her in the van?"

"I don't think so."

"I heard Ashlee's not going," he said.

"Don't sound so happy!"

"Sorry," he said.

"I told her I thought she should go, but she's not listening to anything I say right now. It's funny how she was the one who did something wrong, but now she seems to be the one avoiding me."

"If your enemies are hungry, give them something to eat, and they will be ashamed of what they have done to you."

"What?"

"It's a verse in the Bible," he said. "One of my dad's favorites."

"Oh," she said and laughed. "I like it."

By that afternoon Brianne was so excited about seeing Sarah she could barely stand it. Math and P.E. seemed to drag by. They had to run the mile again, and she felt dead by the end of her four laps around the track, but then she sprinted to the locker room when they were dismissed and couldn't wait to get on the bus.

Austin laughed at her when she sat down.

"Oh, and you aren't excited about seeing Sarah too, Mr. 'Do you think I can sit by her in the van?'"

"Shut up," he said. "I didn't say it like that."

"Yeah right!"

Once the bus pulled away from the school, Brianne had to wait twenty minutes before it came to a stop in front of her driveway, and seeing the Anderson's car parked up by the house made her fly out of the seat and run down the aisle.

"Walk, Brianne," her bus driver reminded her.

"Sorry," she said, stepping past him. "But Sarah's here!"

She didn't bother stopping at the mailbox like she usually did, and she ran all the way up the long driveway, flung the front door open, and stepped inside. Sarah was sitting on the couch with Beth in her lap while her mom and Mrs. Anderson were chatting.

She hurried to her side and gave her a hug around Beth. "You're here!"

Sarah laughed. "I'm here."

"Sarah's here!" she squealed to Beth, giving her a kiss on the forehead.

"Sarah's here," Beth repeated. "I told her you miss her."

"I need to go finish packing," she said, getting up from the couch and heading for her room to change and put the rest of her things into her bags. Sarah came to join her with Beth still in tow.

They talked like old times, and it almost seemed like Sarah had never been gone. Once they were at the school, loading the vans and waiting for everyone to get there, Sarah talked to everyone else too, and they all seemed happy to see her again. Brianne introduced her to Silas and also to Brooke.

"Austin wants to sit by you," she whispered to Sarah when they were trying to decide which van to sit in.

"Do you mind?" Sarah asked.

"No. Do you want to?"

She smiled. "Yeah, I guess. If you're sure it's fine."

"It's fine," she laughed. "I should probably sit with Brooke and Marissa anyway."

"Okay, if we get separated, I'll see you there."

They rode in the same van, but she and Marissa and Brooke were in the back, and Austin and Sarah were in front of them. Marissa had told her she was coming first thing this morning, and Brianne found it a little unbelievable. She had often wanted to invite friends to church who didn't go anywhere, but she wasn't sure how to go about it. But she hadn't planned this at all, and yet Marissa was here.

After they arrived at the camp, they got settled in their room and a bunch of them went for a walk around the lake. At one point she and Sarah had fallen behind the others and had a chance to talk in a more heart-to-heart way than they had thus far.

"When did you invite Marissa to come?"

"Last night," she said. "I can't really say why, but she needed someone to talk to, and she came to youth group and then heard about this."

"Does it have something to do with her mom?"

"Yes. You know about that?"

"She told me once, but I hadn't heard anything about it for awhile."

Brianne also told her how she was doing with forgiving Ashlee, and how things had both changed and stayed the same between herself and Silas.

"He's really cute," Sarah said. "And nice too."

"I know. I can't believe I've become such good friends with him."

"Why?"

"I'm not usually like that with people I've only known for two weeks."

"You were that way with me."

"I know, but you're a girl."

"Do you think Ashlee might have helped in that?"

"As crazy as it sounds, yes. I think maybe she did."

They both laughed.

"All things work together for good, Brianne. Even the ways other people try to hurt us."

***

On Saturday morning Sarah and Brianne had to help with making breakfast, so they got up early and were on the way to the kitchen by seven.

"I think we should work here together someday," Brianne said.

"That would be really fun."

"What would be fun?" Austin asked, coming up behind them on the trail. Apparently he was on K.P. duty this morning too.

"Working here together on summer staff."

"All right. Let's do it," he said.

"I meant me and Sarah," she teased him.

"Ah, come on. You two couldn't be here without me. Admit it."

"We admit it," Sarah said. "Wherever we go, we'll always have you following us around."

Brianne had a fun morning. After breakfast they had group-time with singing, listening to Pastor Doug talk, and then breaking into smaller groups for discussion and prayer, similar to what they did on Thursday nights. She and Sarah were in the same group along with Marissa and some older students. After the meeting they had free-time for about thirty minutes and then met by the lake for a hike. Pastor

Doug led them through the main camp area and up into the hills.

Brianne knew the outlying areas well, picturing where each side trail led to they passed. She and Joel had spent so much time running around these woods together. She was amazed they had never gotten lost, but this was Joel's backyard, so he had always known where they were.

As lunchtime neared, she began to feel more anxious to see him, but after lunch, she faced an unanticipated dilemma. She was heading out of the meeting room toward the lake and Joel's house when Silas' voice stopped her.

"Hey, Brianne. Where are you going?"

She turned back to answer him, supposing he didn't know anything about Joel, but she felt reluctant to tell him.

"I um, was going for a walk," she said, which was sort of true.

"You want some company?"

"Sure," she said, not knowing what else to say. She and Silas walked down to the lake and started walking around its edge. There was an awkward silence between them for a few moments and then Brianne thought of something to talk about.

"How do you like it here?"

"It's nice," he said. "How many times have you been here?"

She laughed. "A lot."

"Like every summer, you mean?"

"Yes, and I used to live close by."

"And you came here a lot?"

"One of my best friends lived here."

"Oh, cool. Does she now?"

Brianne smiled. "It's a he, and yes, he does."

"Where at?"

She looked across the lake and could see the house from where they were. She pointed it out. "Over there. I was on my way to see him, actually."

"Oh," he said. "Sorry. I didn't mean to interrupt your plans."

"You're not. You can come with me. He might not be there right now. I was just going to check."

Silas kept walking with her, and she decided it was fine. She wasn't going just to see Joel anyway. His family would likely be there too. And they were, but Joel wasn't. He had gone fishing with his dad this morning at a nearby river, but they were supposed to be back around two o'clock.

"I told him you were coming today," Megan told her. "So I know he'll be here."

Brianne introduced Silas to Megan and Mrs. West. They seemed a little intrigued by Silas being with her. She told them about his parents work with the American Indian community and their plans to start a church in Clatskanie. But Brianne felt weird having him with her.

On the way back to the retreat center, she told herself once again she wasn't ready for this boy-thing. It felt awkward and complicated. She loved having Silas and Austin and other guys as friends, but anytime it began to feel like something more, she didn't like it.

Chapter Fifteen

"Back so soon?" Sarah asked, looking up from her book.

Brianne sat on the edge of Sarah's bed in the cabin. "He wasn't there. He's coming home around two. I'll go back later."

Sarah gazed at her intently. "What's wrong?"

Brianne bit her lip and tried to hold back the tears. She felt like she had messed everything up with Silas again. She should have told him the truth from the beginning and not invited him to walk with her.

"Oh, sweetie," Sarah said, sitting forward to give her a hug. "What happened?"

Brianne let the tears fall. "I don't know how you do it."

"Do what?"

"Deal with boys."

Sarah laughed. "Most of the time I don't do too well myself. What happened? I thought you said he wasn't there."

"Not Joel. Silas," she said, going on to explain what had happened and how she felt about it. Sarah listened and then told her something she hadn't thought about.

"One thing I try to keep in mind is guys don't know what I'm thinking. You may have felt weird with having Silas there, but he doesn't know that. The Wests aren't important to him like they are to you, so it wasn't an issue for him that you were there together."

"So you don't think I messed everything up?"

"Messed what up? You're just friends."

"I know, but after what happened last week with Ashlee and everything, it's a little more than that, and I thought we were doing fine, but now I feel like it's going to be weird between us again. And I don't want that."

"Then don't let it be. Like I said, Silas doesn't know how you felt, so for him nothing's changed, and if you don't want it to, then keep being the way you've been with him. He won't know the difference unless you start acting weird around him."

Sarah took some red licorice out of her bag and handed her a piece too. Brianne thanked her and took a bite of the sweet treat. She also took a deep breath and let it out, mirroring Sarah's gentle smile.

"I can't do this without you, Sarah."

"Yes, you can."

"No. I can't. Both times something has happened with Silas, I've ended up talking to you about it. What happens when you're not there?"

"God will provide someone else or help you handle it on your own."

They sat there talking for a long time. Sarah told her more about school and the girls she was getting to know. She also had one guy who was pursuing her she had no interest in, and another she did want to be friends with but nothing more at this point, and she was trying to find the balance.

"Are you glad you're here, Sarah? Or are you regretting it now?"

"I'm glad. I'm really glad to be here with you, and I'm enjoying seeing Austin too. I'm going to hide out in here until you get back because I don't want to end up going for a walk with him and giving him the wrong idea, but it is good to see him and everyone else too."

"Is it still okay if I come to your house next weekend?"

"Absolutely. I know you can't spend all your time with me here, and I don't want you to. But next weekend, I'm not sharing you!"

Brianne laughed. "No boys allowed!"

"That's right. Just you and me. We can pretend we're ten all weekend."

Brianne had told Marissa and Brooke she would meet them in the meeting room at three o'clock to do scrapbooking with them, so she knew if she was going to see Joel while she was here, it would have to be now.

Heading back around the lake, all alone this time, she didn't make it to the house before she spotted him. He was out in the front yard playing fetch with his dog, tossing a tennis ball into an adjacent field and waiting for Sam to return it. He'd had Sam for a couple of years now, she realized. He had gotten him for his tenth birthday shortly before she moved.

He saw her coming and came to meet her, not hesitating for a second to give her a hug, which she welcomed easily. He was even with her in height. Most guys her age were shorter than her right now with the exception of Austin whose thirteenth birthday was next month.

Joel grabbed her hand and pulled her toward the forest beyond the house. "Come on, I have something to show you," he said with an excited twinkle in his brown eyes.

She walked with him for a few paces until he dropped her hand and broke into a jog. She kept up with him until they reached the trail, and then she reminded him she wasn't a distance runner or a country girl anymore. The farthest she had to walk at a quick pace was from her locker to the band room and back every day.

"You need some muscle on those legs, girl. They're like toothpicks."

"I know," she laughed. "You should see me run the mile. By the end I feel like they're going to snap."

It didn't take them too long to reach their destination, and it wasn't anything like what she was expecting. She thought he had made some kind of discovery like the eagle's nest last summer, but this was something he was making—a lookout tower overlooking the camp.

"Is it safe?" she asked halfway up the sturdy but tall ladder.

"Yes. Just don't look down," he said from above her. "Eventually I'll have this all enclosed so it will be safe enough for campers to use, but for now hang on and don't try to go too fast."

If it had been anyone but Joel leading her, she never would have gone, but she trusted him. She tried not to think about having to climb down after they got to the top. When she reached the landing, she was glad to see it had a temporary but secure guardrail around it, and she was glad she hadn't let her fears keep her on the ground. It was an incredible view.

"Joel! How did you know to build it right here? This is amazing."

He smiled. "I was climbing that tree one day this summer," he said pointing to the one directly behind them, "and I saw the view and knew I had to find a way to see it without having to climb the tree like that."

"I can see why," she laughed, not able to imagine how he had climbed such a tall tree, let alone build something like this. "You're amazing."

She looked at the view once again and let her eyes scan the lake, fields, buildings, and trees of the beautiful setting, suddenly feeling very homesick for this place and wishing they had never moved away.

Joel sat down on the wide platform, and she joined him, talking to him for quite some time about her current life, her family, her best friend moving away, and the new friends she had made.

"Sarah's here this weekend, so that's been fun. I miss her, but I can see God filling in the gaps and giving me whatever I need when I need it."

"Sarah's here and you're spending time with me?"

"You were my best friend before I moved up there. I miss you too."

"You and Sarah have to work here during the summer when we're old enough. Then you could have all summer with both of us."

"I know. We were talking about that this morning. That would be so fun. I can't wait!"

"I thought you said you wished we could stay ten forever?"

"Or that we could jump to sixteen. That has to be better than being twelve."

He laughed. "What's so bad about being twelve?"

She told him what Ashlee had done to her last week, feeling a little embarrassed about having a conversation about a boy with Joel, simply because she had never done so before. But Joel listened and said something she hadn't considered.

"Megan had something like that happen to her this summer. One of her friends knew she liked somebody, and her friend told him right in front of Megan and a bunch of other people. She's seventeen. I don't think that stuff goes away because we get older."

"Thanks, I feel so much better now."

He laughed. "Don't worry about it, Brianne. Don't become like a bunch of girls in my youth group who are obsessed with how they look and which boys like them. It's stupid. We're twelve."

She smiled. Joel reminded her of Silas in a way, and she recalled the way Silas had looked when he accepted her false invitation to the dance.

"And what would you do if a girl you liked wrote you a note that said, 'I really like you and think you're super-cute. Will you go to the dance with me?'"

"I don't think that will ever happen."

"Why not?"

"Because I'm not the one girls are always pointing at and whispering about."

"And what about the other girls?"

"What other girls?"

"The ones who aren't like that. The ones who come to church every week but sit quietly and read a book like my friend Emily or are actually there to learn about God and grow closer to Him like Sarah?"

He shrugged. "I guess I haven't noticed."

She laughed. "I guarantee they've noticed you, Joel West."

He looked embarrassed and stood to his feet. "Well, they're going to have to wait, because right now I have more important things to do, like finish this tower and pass the seventh grade."

Brianne stood up, and they looked at the view once again. She tried to imagine what Joel would look like when he was seventeen and began looking at girls differently than he did now. If he had started coming to her school and she had connected with him like she had done with Silas, she could imagine herself liking him in a similar way. He was cute, nice, and someone she felt comfortable being around.

"What time is it?" she asked, seeing Joel had a watch on.

"Three o'clock," he said.

She was surprised they had been up here so long. "I need to go," she said. "My friends are going to wonder what happened to me."

"Okay," he said, leading the way to the opening in the platform where the ladder was. He went down first and then waited for her. "Don't look down," he laughed.

"Too late," she said, feeling queasy.

"It's all right. You can do it toothpick-girl."

She swung her legs over the edge and placed her foot on the ladder, then hung on for dear life until she was halfway down and she no longer had visions of slipping and plummeting thirty feet to the ground.

They walked back to his house, and she expected to say good-bye to him there, but he kept walking with her all the way to the other side of the lake.

"Do you want to hang out with us?" she asked, not wanting to say good-bye to him so soon. She had been looking forward to this for a month, and now it was over.

"No. I already attract enough girls in my own youth group. I don't need to be adding any more to the list."

She laughed. "Not all of my friends are girls. And you would like Austin and Silas."

"Not this time," he said. "But I am glad you're here and you came to spend time with me."

"I'm glad too," she said, turning to face him and giving him a hug. "I've missed you."

"I've missed you too, Brianne. Maybe one of these years we can have more than an hour to run around in these woods together again."

"I'd like that," she said. "Make that ladder less scary by next summer, and I'll sit up there with you and share about my latest adventures in the junior high world."

"Promise?"

"Yes," she said, wondering why he sounded skeptical.

"Even if you've got a boyfriend by then?"

"I won't have a boyfriend by then," she said. "I'm waiting until I'm sixteen."

"Promise?"

Now he reminded her of Austin—that protective, big brother side of him that always surprised her. But this was the first time she had seen it in Joel.

"I promise," she said.

"Are you one of those girls who whispers and points at cute guys or who hides behind a book?"

She laughed. "I think somewhere in between."

"That's good, Brianne. Stay that way, okay?"

"Okay. And no falling for a girl with perfect hair unless she can quote at least five Bible verses and actually lives by them."

"No worries about that," he said.

"I think you might be surprised."

"I'm not ready to be surprised yet. I'll keep working on that ladder for you—the only girl I plan on being up there with for a few more years."

"Promise?"

"Yes. I definitely promise."

She smiled and turned away, telling him good-bye and asking him to write her once in a while. He never returned her letters.

Going to the cabin, she got her scrapbooking stuff and headed for the meeting room where Sarah, Marissa, Emily, and Brooke were waiting for her. She knew she was later than she said, and she wasn't surprised when they asked why she had been gone so long.

She told them about the tower Joel was building, which of course they wanted to go see, but she said they should wait until next summer when it was safer for all of them to be up there.

They had begun to work on their individual projects when Austin and Silas wandered into the room. Austin sat beside Sarah and asked her what she was working on. She was putting together a friendship scrapbook of all of her friends in Clatskanie, and Austin seemed surprised she had made a page about him.

"Did you get to see Joel, Brianne?" Austin asked.

"Yes."

"He took her to his tree fort," Emily said.

"Shut up," she laughed. "It's not a tree fort. It's a lookout tower."

"Okay, let's leave Brianne alone," Sarah said. "If she says Joel is just a good friend, we should believe her."

Brianne felt grateful for Sarah's intervention and not that surprised when no one else said anything on the matter. Sarah had the ability to lead others to do the right thing without being bossy.

Brianne realized she had left one of her packets of pictures in the room. She had taken it out of her bag earlier to show Sarah photos from the barbecue. Getting up from her chair, she headed to the cabin, got the pictures from her top bunk, and headed back to the meeting room. Silas was waiting for her outside the door.

"Hey, Brianne. Can I talk to you?" he asked.

"Sure."

"I um, I just wanted to apologize about what happened earlier."

"When?"

"When I went over to your friend's house with you. I shouldn't have done that."

Okay, what do I say here? I don't want to make it out to be a big deal, but I don't want to lie either. What would Sarah say?

"He wasn't there anyway, so it didn't matter."

"I know, but if he would have been, that probably would have been awkward for you."

"Why do you think that?"

"It wouldn't have been?"

Okay, Brianne, stop trying to avoid the issue and be honest.

"Yes. I guess you're right. Joel is a really good friend and I wouldn't want him to think me and you are boyfriend and girlfriend or anything, because we're not, right?"

"Right."

"But I could have told him that. It's not like I don't want to be seen with you because of what other people think. As long as you and I are being honest with each other about what we both want, that's what matters."

"Okay," he said. "I just wanted to make sure you weren't mad at me because next to Austin, you're kind of the best friend I have right now."

"And your new neighbor."

"Yes, that too."

She smiled at him and suddenly felt very comfortable. She had prayed for two things when Sarah had moved away: for a new best friend, and for good neighbors like the Andersons had been. And now, a month later, she had several friends who by themselves weren't quite like Sarah, but all together they were filling up her life in much the same way; and she had definitely ended up with great neighbors. She could imagine having a lot of fun times with Silas, and he was becoming one of her best friends too.

Chapter Sixteen

On Saturday evening after dinner, the whole group played a game requiring a lot of teamwork to accomplish. Brianne was in a group that made it fun, and she felt much closer to her teammates when it was over. Some were ones she already knew well, and others she barely knew, like older high school students she hadn't connected with yet.

One of the most memorable moments was when she, Sarah, and Austin had to be blindfolded and walk on the path beside the lake with their legs tied together in three-legged race fashion, only in this case it was a four-legged race where they had to coordinate their steps and also follow Marissa's verbal instructions about where to walk to avoid falling into the lake.

They didn't fall in, but Brianne stepped into the water a couple of times. That got her pants wet, and another part of the game got them dirty. After they were finished playing, she and Sarah went back to the cabin to change their clothes before the evening meeting.

Pastor Doug had been talking about relationships this weekend—everything from friendships, to dating, to relating to those who don't know God, and she felt like she was doing okay in some areas and needed to improve in others. But tonight he said something that really hit home for her.

"The most important relationships we will ever have are those in our own family. Sometimes it's easier to focus on outside relationships: friendships, someone you're dating, or even people you don't know well. I spent a lot of years trying to invest time and energy into youth group kids and other people who needed my practical help or guidance, and by the time I got home I didn't have much left for my family. But I've changed that. I've made the relationships in my home the priority, and I believe that's the way it should be.

"Now none of you are married and have kids yet, but you do have parents and siblings, and I'm going to ask you a question: How much effort are you putting into those relationships compared to others you have?"

He gave them time to think, and Brianne knew she was doing okay in some ways, like she generally listened to her parents and didn't get into big arguments with them, and she tried to be a good big sister to Steven and Beth because they were special, but her own natural brothers she wasn't as loving and forgiving with. And up until recently when Sarah had moved away, she had spent more time with Sarah than all of her siblings put together. Sarah had often suggested coming to her house instead, but she would always say, 'No, your house is quieter. If you come here, we'll be interrupted every two minutes.'

"God has placed you in your family for a reason," Pastor Doug went on. "Some of those reasons have to do with others being there for you and meeting your needs, but He also has a purpose for you to be there for them: to love them, to bring joy to their lives, to be a good example for your younger brothers and sisters, to teach or encourage them in some way. Don't just take from your family, but learn to give too. They will be blessed by it, and so will you.

"I know some of you are saying, 'I have an awful family, Pastor Doug. I can't stand being around them. My parents fight all the time, or my step dad hates me, or my brother is mean to me. And I sympathize with that. No family is perfect and some are a complete wreck, but they're still your family and you need to do everything you can to be a good part of it. But you can't do that in your own strength and wisdom; you need God to lead you, and He will if you ask Him to."

On the worksheet they filled out during their small-group time, Brianne wrote some practical ways she could invest more time and love into her family. Spending more time with them was at the top of the list, along with helping her mom more around the house, helping her brothers with their homework after school instead of only getting hers done, and going to her parents more for advice and direction instead of trying to solve problems herself. They were always helpful when she went to them, but sometimes that was her last choice instead of her first.

After the meeting they went to the campfire area to have s'mores, sing, and have a silent prayer time, and she asked God for help in being a loving daughter and sister, and she also asked Him for help in being a good friend to several of the people who were surrounding her.

"You okay?" Sarah asked on the way back to the cabin. Their friends were around them, but they had a little space at the moment.

"I'm thinking about what Pastor Doug was saying about having good relationships with our family members. I feel like I could do better in that."

"Me too," Sarah said. "But I liked what he said about my relationship with God being the key to success in any other relationships I have. I need to have that first before I can even think about being a good friend or having a boyfriend or loving my family more."

"Hey, what happened to not having a boyfriend until you're sixteen?" she whispered. "Did something happen with you and Austin today you're not telling me?"

She laughed. "No, silly. And that gives me four years to get really solid with Jesus so when that time comes, I can be more ready to enter the dating world."

"That makes sense," she said. "You're brilliant, Sarah. By the time you're sixteen, you're going to be exactly like Megan."

"Who's Megan?"

"Thumper. Our counselor here this summer?"

"Oh, right. I just know her as Thumper."

"One reason I wish Silas wouldn't have been with me when I went over to the house today is because I would have liked to stay and talked to her more, but it was too weird with him there. I'm going to have to write her when I get home and let her know he's not my boyfriend."

"Have you talked to him since then?"

"Oh yeah, I forgot to tell you. He came and talked to me and apologized for going there with me. I'm not sure how he knew that made me uncomfortable, but he did, and I had a chance to let him know it really doesn't matter to me what other people think as long as we're honest with each other."

"See! You know how to handle it."

"Yeah, I guess so. I think that's where my relationship with God comes in. I've been praying about the whole thing since Ashlee wrote him that note. And so far, He's helped everything work out okay, much better than I would have imagined last week."

In the morning they had breakfast, followed by a time they were supposed to have some individual quiet time with God by finding a place where they could be alone, read their Bibles, pray, and think about what God had been teaching them this weekend.

It was cold outside, so Brianne decided to go back to the cabin and have her time with Jesus on her bunk. Several other girls chose that option too, but they were all quiet and left each other alone. Brianne read over the verses from their discussion sheet last night. She felt God speaking to her heart in a similar way about focusing on her family more, and also about what Sarah had said about getting to know God better and focusing on her relationship with Him if she wanted to improve her relationships with her family and be a good friend.

They had been told the time they were supposed to be back in the main meeting room, and she was about to head that way when Marissa came over to her bunk and asked if she could talk to her. Marissa had been lying on her own bed, and Brianne thought maybe she was sleeping, but once they were outside, Marissa told her what she had really been doing.

"I've been thinking a lot about what Pastor Doug said on the first night and yesterday morning about having a relationship with God, and I guess I don't really understand what he means by that. Can you explain it to me?"

"Sure," she said, feeling a little unsure about where to begin. "I can try anyway." God was very real to her, and she believed in Him, but it was a heart-thing more than something she could explain with words.

"I guess I basically believe God made all of us and the world, but He's more than someone out there who's really powerful and beyond our reach. He also loves us very much and wants us to know Him and depend on Him."

"But how can we know Him if we can't see Him or hear Him?"

"That's what the Bible is for. It teaches us about God and what He's like and how He wants us to live. And we can talk to God and hear Him when we pray, but just like inside our hearts. I can't really explain it, but I know it's real because I feel it—I feel Jesus with me."

Marissa seemed to get what she was saying, and she asked her something else. "And how does that help you? I mean, what difference does it make whether you know God or not?"

Brianne had to think about that. What difference did knowing God make in her life?

"You know that thing that happened with Ashlee where she put a note in Silas' locker?"

"Yeah."

"That made me really mad, and I was so embarrassed, and I didn't know how to act normal around Silas after that, so I prayed about it. I asked God to help me, and He did in several different ways:

"First Silas came to talk to me, and I was able to be honest with him about how I really felt. And then Sarah called me that afternoon and I talked to her about it. God helped me to forgive Ashlee, even though I didn't want to, and now it's like I can leave it behind and move on. I know I wouldn't have been able to do that without God's help. I'd still be mad and embarrassed, but I'm not."

"Could God help me deal with my mom making herself sick and other stuff that's hard?"

"Yes. He hears us when we pray, and He will help us and guide us if we're looking for that."

"And what about Jesus? Who's that? The guy I pray to?"

"Jesus is God. He came to earth to die for our sins so we can know Him and have eternal life. He's in heaven now and all around us, and He also lives in our hearts when we ask Him to. He forgives us for the bad stuff we've done and then is with us all the time to help us make the right choices. You can call Him God, or Jesus, or Lord, but it's all the same. The God who made us and loves us. The only real God there is."

Marissa didn't ask anything else, and Brianne decided to ask her if she wanted to pray right now and take the first step in getting to know God. Marissa said she did, and Brianne told her to tell God whatever was on her heart. That He was listening, and all she had to do was believe it and ask Him to be in her life, and He would be.

Chapter Seventeen

Marissa closed her eyes and prayed out loud. Brianne held her hand and listened.

"God, I feel like my life is such a mess. My mom is sick again, and it seems like she just gets worse, not better, and I don't know how to deal with that. I don't understand why she keeps doing this, but I know I've done a lot of things lately I know aren't right either. But it's easier to hang out with my friends and go along with whatever they're doing than to be at home sometimes.

"I look at Brianne and wish I was like her. I wish I could have a family like she has. I wish I could be a good person all the time like she is, but she tells me you're the reason her family is what it is, and that she knows you and that helps her. I want that too, God. I want to know who you are, and hear you telling me what to do, and have you help me to understand my mom and not give up hope that she can get better. I don't understand everything about you, but I want to. Please help me. Make yourself real to me like the way you are to Brianne."

She stopped talking but started to cry. Brianne pulled her close and held her for a long time, and she felt amazed Marissa had come to her like this, asked her some questions, and then prayed like she couldn't wait another second.

Once Marissa stopped crying, Brianne went inside to get her some tissue and then returned, asking her if she was all right and if she had any more questions.

"I'm sure I do, but I can't think of any right now," she said. "Sorry, I didn't expect to be so emotional about it."

"It's all right. I'm glad you asked, and that's what this group is for. All of us are doing the same thing with trying to get to know God better, and you can know Him like I do, Mar, and it really does make a difference."

"I know. I can feel it already. That was like, 'Wow! I'm not alone. My life can make sense! There is a God and He loves me, and I don't have to feel so alone anymore.'"

Brianne smiled, and Marissa's words were a good reminder for her. Her seventh grade year had gotten off to an interesting start. Some good, some bad, and some she wasn't sure how to feel about yet. But God was with her, and He could help her with whatever she faced in the future, just like He had been doing so far.

On the ride home that afternoon she sat beside Sarah until they dropped her off in Portland, and then she sat beside Silas, and she had a good time talking to him and getting to know him better. They both talked about their lives up to this point, and Brianne realized they had a lot in common besides having dads who were pastors. They'd also both had to move and leave friends behind. She had lost a good friend in Sarah this year, but God had filled the void with some new friends, and Silas was experiencing the same since moving here and leaving his friends behind in California.

She told him about her desire to focus more time and effort into her family instead of always wanting to be with her friends, and he had thought about the same thing. He seemed thoughtful after that and turned quiet, and she knew he was probably thinking about his sister, so she left him alone and wondered what that would be like to see one of her siblings living a destructive kind of life and pushing God out of it.

Saying good-bye to Silas and everyone else after they arrived at the church, she put her things into the van and they took Marissa home. Marissa gave her a hug before she went inside, and Brianne told her she could talk anytime and would be praying for her.

Once she and her dad were back on the road, Brianne told him about Marissa praying to invite Jesus into her life after asking her some questions this morning.

"That's great, sweetheart," he said. "I'm very proud of you."

"I don't think it was me," she said. "She just started asking me questions, and it all spilled out. I think I understand God better now too."

When they got home, her dad had something for her and brought it into her room when she was unpacking. She took the shopping bag from him and looked inside, pulling out the wire-bound book and reading the title. It was a devotional book for teen girls called, *Heaven In My Heart.*

"I know you've been interested in reading your Bible more and growing in your relationship with God, and I thought this might help you in that."

"Thanks, Daddy," she said, giving him a hug.

Of all the things God had brought to her attention this weekend, the thing that remained foremost on her mind was her desire to cherish her family more. Sarah had given her something when she said good-bye to her in Portland. It was a letter, and she told her not to read it until she got home. She wanted to read it now, but Beth was being extra-clingy after her being gone for three days and her mom wanted to hear about her weekend, so she went back out to the living room and joined the rest of her family.

They went out for pizza after she shared about her weekend, and when they returned she needed to finish the last of her homework, but she also read several books to Beth before bed and then left the room to let her sleep. Going to find her mom, she wanted to ask her something she had been thinking about ever since saying good-bye to Sarah this afternoon.

"Mom?"

"Yes, honey?" her mom said, looking up from the pile of laundry she was folding.

Brianne stepped over to help and then asked her question. "Would it be all right if you came and picked me up on Saturday next weekend instead of Sunday?"

"Sure," she said, sounding concerned. "Is everything okay between you and Sarah?"

"Yeah, everything's fine. I was just thinking since I got to see her this weekend, and I'll probably need time to do homework, it might be better if I stayed one night instead of two."

"That's fine. Whatever you want to do."

Brianne remained in the bedroom and finished helping her mom with folding her brothers' clothes and then helped her put them away. After they were finished, her mom thanked her and gave her a hug. Brianne hung on and felt thankful for her mom's love and all she did for her and her siblings.

She was about to step away and go back to her room to finally have a chance to read Sarah's letter when her mom asked her something.

"Did you see the Wests while you were there?"

"Yes. I saw everyone except Dave. He was fishing with Joel when I stopped by the first time, and then when I went back to see Joel, I didn't go inside."

"Did you have a nice visit with them?"

She smiled, remembering the awkwardness of having Silas with her the first time. She decided to go ahead and tell her mom that because she would probably get questioned by Mrs. West about it the next time they talked on the phone.

"It's funny now," she said when her mom laughed and she did also, "but at the time I was like, 'Why did I let him follow me here? They're going to think he's my boyfriend!' I'm really glad Joel wasn't there."

"And how is Joel?"

"The same. He's building this really cool lookout tower. It was about thirty feet off the ground, and I can't believe I climbed all the way up there, but the view was amazing. Are we going to visit them sometime soon?"

"I don't know. Your dad and I have talked about it, but we haven't made any definite plans. Maybe we'll go there for Thanksgiving since we're going to Washington for Christmas this year."

Both sets of her grandparents lived in Washington along with most of her aunts, uncles, and cousins. Her mom had grown up in Bellingham, and her dad was from Seattle. They usually went there for either Thanksgiving or Christmas and then during the summer for a week or two. She was looking forward to seeing her grandparents and a couple of cousins who were her age, and she thought it would be great if they went to the camp for Thanksgiving. She would like to have more time with Megan and see Joel again before next summer.

She didn't read Sarah's letter until after she got into bed. She took her new devotional book along with her Bible from her night stand and planned to get started on that tonight, but she read Sarah's letter first.

Dear Brianne,

I'm really glad I decided to come this weekend, and I'm looking forward to seeing you in another week too, but I'm also beginning to see why God may be separating us for a time. You were really different this weekend than I've ever seen you. You've always been a nice person and friendly to everyone, but I could see you have deepened your relationships with Austin, Emily, and Marissa over this past month as well as forming two new friendships with Silas and Brooke. Something tells me that wouldn't have happened if I was still in Clatskanie, and for their sake I'm glad, because they all have a great friend in you, and I think this is God's way of showing me I was hogging you too much!

But I also think you and me can actually become closer than ever now that distance separates us. I really enjoyed talking to you about your relationship with God and mine, and I know we didn't do that much before. When we thought we had all the time in the world, we focused on superficial things a lot, but when we know we have to fit everything into a two-page letter or ten-minute phone call, or a weekend, we skip all the things that don't matter so much and speak more from our hearts. Don't you think?

I may be living apart from you now, but I want you to know I still see you as my best friend, and I hope you see me that way too. Always feel free to share whatever is on your mind and heart with me, and I will do the same in return.

Love you,
Sarah

Brianne took some stationery from her drawer and responded to the letter right away, telling Sarah she'd had a great weekend with her too and that she agreed with what she was saying about their relationship being different now, but better in some ways. She also told her about her plans to only stay until Saturday next weekend and explaining why, and she told her about the new devotional book her dad had given her and said she would be sharing with her what she learned.

If you don't hear anything, that will either mean I haven't been doing it or that I'm just not sharing, so be nosy and ask me about it. I'm planning to keep putting more effort into the friendships I have here and the relationships with my family, but I know I'll do much better with both of those if I'm letting God fill up more of my mind and heart and growing closer than ever to Jesus.

Have a great day and know I'm thinking of you and praying for you. And you're still my best friend too—even from a distance.

Always,
Brianne

I love to hear from my readers

Write me at:

living_loved@yahoo.com

Titles in the Heaven in my Heart series:

Closer Than Ever
Anything You Need
A Real Friend
Don't Let Go
Face To Face
Keeping It Real
By Your Side
Let It Shine